LUIGI FERRO
SHE WANTED TO DANCE

Luigi Ferro
She Wanted to Dance
Story by Matt Borne
Copyright © 2023
Cover by Mats Ingelborn
Photos by A.Karnaushenko, Kiuikson & Wirestock
ISBN print: 978-91-89822-45-0
ISBN e-book: 978-91-89822-46-7
Published by Yabot AB, Sweden, 2024

1

The sun was setting over San Marino, casting its golden light on the ancient city walls as I walked the labyrinthine streets of the old city. I greeted the locals with casual nods and brief exchanges, maintaining the facade of the approachable and friendly neighborhood detective. In truth, my mind was always working, observing the slightest shift in expressions or tone of voice, filing away information for future use.

I caught my own reflection as I passed a big shop window. I looked at my attire, a tailored suit that hugged my frame like a lover's embrace, and the polished leather shoes that clicked on the worn street. My dark hair and beard, trimmed to a fashionable 3 millimeters, completed the image of the suave private investigator I had become.

"Buonasera, Signor Ferro," called out the butcher, as I passed his shop.

"Buonasera, Angelo," I replied, nodding at him while noting the faint traces of blood under his fingernails.

"Did you hear about the break-in last night?" he asked, looking troubled.

"Si, but don't worry, they'll be caught," I assured him, suppressing the urge to ask more questions. Work was never far from my mind.

"Ah, you're right," he said, his face brightening. "You always find the truth, Signor Ferro."

"Only when it wants to be found," I muttered under

my breath as I continued on my way, keenly aware of the shadows that seemed to grow darker with each passing hour.

The world around me was a web of secrets and lies, but I relished the challenge of untangling them, exposing the hidden cracks that would bring the guilty to justice. It was this passion that had driven me to become a private investigator in the first place, and it burned within me like an unquenchable flame.

As the night settled over San Marino, I couldn't help but feel the weight of the darkness that lay beneath its beauty, ready to reveal itself at any moment. But, as long as I drew breath, I would continue to seek out the truth, no matter how well it hid or how deep it burrowed.

The sun's last rays disappeared behind the mountains as I slowed my steps in front of a weathered building and stepped into the dimly lit interior of Bar Della Rocca, seeking refuge from the encroaching night. The scent of strong coffee mingled with the musty aroma of old books and well-worn leather, creating an atmosphere that was both comforting and mysterious.

"Ah, Signor Ferro," called out the bartender, greeting me with a nod as he polished a glass. "The usual?"

"Per favore," I replied, taking my seat at the bar and allowing my eyes to roam over the patrons gathered in hushed conversations.

I sipped my gin with a twist of lime, watching the world go by with half-closed eyes. This little ritual always allowed me to forget, if only for a moment, the darkness that lurked beneath the surface of this picturesque town.

It wasn't long before she arrived—Caterina. She sauntered into the room, her heels clicking against the stone floor like a metronome. Her hair was a waterfall of chestnut curls that framed her face and cascaded down her back. The electric blue dress she wore clung to her every curve, its neckline plunging dangerously low. She caught my eye and smirked, knowing full well the effect she had on me.

"Buonasera, Luigi," she purred, sliding onto the stool next to mine. "Fancy seeing you here."

"Is it so surprising, Caterina?" I asked, taking a sip of my freshly poured gin. "This is one of the few places in town where I can escape the judgmental stares."

"True," she conceded, signaling for the bartender to pour her a glass of red wine. "But I thought after our last encounter you might be keeping your distance."

I looked into her dark, almond-shaped eyes and let out a soft chuckle. "You know me better than that, cara mia. Besides, I find it hard to resist temptation when it's staring me in the face."

"Ah, temptation," she sighed, tapping a finger against the rim of her wine glass. "That's always been your weakness, hasn't it?"

"Is that so?" I asked with a raised eyebrow, my mind drifting back to past cases where desire had led me down dangerous paths. The memory of a high-stakes poker game in Venice, an affair with a femme fatale, and the sting of betrayal still lingered like old wounds.

"Si, Luigi," she continued, leaning closer and

brushing her fingers against my forearm. "But then again, you wouldn't be the man you are today without those dalliances."

"Perhaps not," I admitted, feeling the warmth of her touch seeping into my skin. "It's true that some of my most challenging cases have been driven by passion or greed. But, as a detective, I've learned to keep my desires in check. It's the only way to maintain focus and see the truth."

"Ah, the truth," Caterina mused, tilting her head to one side. "Such an elusive creature, isn't it? Always hiding in the shadows, waiting for someone like you to drag it into the light."

"Indeed," I agreed, swirling the ice in my glass. "But it's a pursuit that never loses its thrill, no matter how many times I've tasted victory or faced defeat."

"Spoken like a true detective," she whispered, her lips brushing against my ear. "And yet, here you sit, drowning your sorrows in gin. Has the chase finally caught up with you, mio amore?"

"Only when I allow it to," I murmured, my voice heavy with the weight of unspoken memories. "The darkness can be seductive, Caterina, but I refuse to let it consume me."

"Bravo," she applauded softly, raising her wine glass in a toast. "To the eternal dance of truth and temptation."

"Salute," I replied, clinking my glass against hers. "May we never lose our footing."

I drained the last drops of my gin, feeling the cold glass against my lips, and observed the people of San

Marino preparing to end their day. I saw Caterina following the flow out of the bar, admiring her shapely behind disappearing in the night. The rhythm of life pulsed slowly through the town, oblivious to the secrets and mysteries hidden beneath the surface. My gaze fell upon a man approaching me with heavy footsteps, his face etched with lines of worry and despair.

"Signor Ferro," he began, his voice thick with a slavic accent, "I am told you are the man to see when in need of help."

"Depends on the kind of help you're looking for," I replied, my eyes never leaving his. I could tell from his stocky build and kind brown eyes that this man was no stranger to hardship. He had the look of a father who would go to any lengths to protect his child.

"My daughter, Elena, she is missing," he said, wringing his hands together anxiously. "She came to Italy to pursue her dream of becoming a dancer. But now… I've lost all contact with her."

He presented himself as Mr. Popescu from Romania, and as he started to spill his story his eyes, clouded with worry, searched mine for a glimmer of hope.

"Elena, she's always been passionate about dancing," he continued, his voice tinged with pride. "Since she was a little girl in our small Romanian village, she'd dance to any tune, her laughter as bright as her steps. Two months ago, she moved to Venice, drawn by its vibrant arts scene." He sighed heavily, the lines on his face deepening. "She used to call every week, her voice bubbling over with stories of rehearsals and new friends. But two weeks ago, the calls just... stopped." His hands clenched into fists.

"I've tried everything, Signor Ferro, but it's like she's vanished into thin air."

"Have you contacted the police?" I asked, my mind already beginning to catalog the potential avenues of investigation.

"Yes, but they have done nothing!" Mr. Popescu's frustration was palpable. "They say she is an adult and must have just run off or gotten lost. But I know my Elena. She would never do such a thing."

"Mr. Popescu," I hesitated, my thoughts swirling like the ice in my empty glass. "Missing persons cases can be… challenging. There's often not much to go on and the trail can quickly grow cold."

"Please, Signore," he implored, desperation lacing his words. "You are my last hope. I have heard of your skills as a detective. If anyone can find my Elena, it is you. And I have brought my life savings…" He took a thick envelope from his pocket and placed it before me.

I studied the man in front of me, weighed down by the burden of worry and fear for his daughter. I thought back to the many cases I had solved, the ghosts of both victory and defeat haunting my every step. Yet, there was something about the raw honesty in Mr. Popescu's eyes that tugged at my sense of justice.

"Alright," I finally agreed, standing up from my chair. "I'll take the case."

"Thank you, Signor Ferro," he breathed, relief flooding his features. "I am forever in your debt."

"Let's not get ahead of ourselves," I cautioned, my

voice firm but not unkind. "First, we need to find Elena. And to do that, I'll need everything you can give me – photos, information, anything that might lead us to her."

"Of course, I will provide you with everything," Mr. Popescu assured me, determination burning in his eyes.

*

Rain was drumming a steady rhythm against the small attic window of my office, casting a melancholy backdrop to the cobblestone streets of San Marino. I heard the creak of the narrow staircase as a visitor made his way up, each step groaning under his considerable weight. The musty scent of old wood and long-forgotten tales wafted through the air, mingling with the faint aroma of espresso from my machine.

My office, tucked away in a corner of San Marino's illustrious Piazza della Libertà, was a far cry from the grandeur of its address. It was a modest space, barely accommodating a cluttered desk, an old leather sofa whose once-luxurious sheen had faded, and a filing cabinet that had long lost its battle with time. I sat perched on the edge of my desk, a cup of espresso in hand, as Mr. Popescu entered. In my cramped office, with its lingering smell of old tobacco and lost stories, he seemed like a bear that had unwittingly stumbled into a bird's nest. His broad, towering frame made the room feel even smaller, dwarfing the modest assortment of furniture.

He sat down opposite me, his hands, rough and calloused, fidgeting in his lap.

"As I told you last night, my daughter, Elena, is missing," he began, his voice thick with an accent from rural Romania. "She went to Italy, to fulfill her dream of dancing in Venice."

I listened, keeping my face neutral but attentive. Parents looking for missing children were a common sight in my line of work, but Popescu's raw, unfiltered emotion struck a chord.

"Elena was the life of our village," he continued, his gaze drifting towards the rain-blurred window. "She'd dance at every festival, enchanting everyone. But two weeks ago, her letters, her calls... they just stopped. Elena always kept in touch, always."

I took a sip of my espresso, letting its warmth and aroma fill me for a moment.

"Did she mention any friends in Venice? Someone she was particularly close to?" I asked, already piecing together a starting point in my mind.

He shook his head. "Just her fellow dancers and some artists she met. She lived with other dancers near Marghera. That's all I know."

I scribbled down the name – Marghera. A lead, at least.

"And her dance company? What did they say?"

"They thought she'd come back to Romania. She hadn't been to rehearsals for weeks before I called them," he replied, frustration lacing his voice.

I placed my cup down, feeling the familiar stir of intrigue. A missing dancer, sudden silence, and a dance company in the dark – it was a puzzle, and puzzles were what I lived for.

"Don't worry, Mr. Popescu," I said firmly, meeting his gaze. "I'll find out what happened to Elena. I'll go to Venezia to find out what's happened."

Relief and a father's tormented hope flickered across Popescu's face. He nodded, clasping his hands tightly, clinging to that sliver of hope.

I watched him leave, the rain outside growing heavier, like nature's own tears. The mystery of Elena's disappearance cast a shadow over the quaint beauty of San Marino, and I was set on uncovering the truth beneath it.

2

Venice was a far cry from the quiet cobblestone streets of San Marino. The moment I set foot on Venetian soil, I could feel the city's pulse throbbing under my soles like a living entity. Venice was a seductress, luring me into her labyrinth of narrow alleys and winding canals, whispering promises of secrets that lay hidden beneath her shimmering waters. It was as if she knew why I was here, why I had left behind the tranquil streets of San Marino and ventured into her sensual embrace.

"Luigi Ferro," I whispered to myself, drawing in a deep breath of the city's salt-laden air, thick and intoxicating as a lover's heady perfume. "This time, you're truly in the thick of it." The words hung heavy in my mind, echoing the daunting complexity of the task ahead.

Elena's disappearance had led me to this city of masks, where truth and deception danced together in a tantalizing tango. With each step I took on the ancient cobblestones, I felt the weight of history press against me, reminding me of the countless souls who had walked these paths before me, seeking answers, seeking solace, seeking redemption.

As I navigated the maze of Venice, I found myself drawn to the pulsating heart of the city's artistic community. I could hear it beating in the rhythm of a thousand footsteps echoing through the piazzas, in the laughter of aspiring artists sharing dreams over glasses of wine, and in the mournful melodies of street musicians serenading the sunlit canals.

I needed to learn more about her connections in the city's artistic underworld. Who were these poets, painters, and dancers she had been spending her nights with?

My first stop was Palazzo della Danza, the baroque palace where Elena took dance classes. I hoped someone there could shed light on her social circle.

The grandeur of the building contrasted with the shabby dancers I found rehearsing inside. A group of lithe dancers practiced at the barre, extending their lean limbs in graceful arcs and bends.

The instructor, a slender woman with her dark hair pulled back in a tight bun, eyed me warily as I approached.

"What do you want?" she asked, fixing my gaze with dark, hard eyes.

"Excuse me, signorina," I said, trying a friendly smile. "I'm looking for information about a young woman named Elena Popescu. I believe she came here to pursue her dreams as a dancer."

At the mention of her name, the instructor's gaze softened.

"Ah, Elena," she replied, pausing for a moment. "A beautiful girl with eyes like emeralds and a spirit that danced even when her feet were still. She was always eager to learn, to grow, to soar. Such passion," she mused.

She said Elena had immediately been drawn into

Venice's thriving artistic community - late nights spent in smoky cafes discussing art and philosophy with dancers, painters, and poets.

"She was seeking something here," the instructor said. "A type of freedom. But this city...it can also be dangerous for a young girl alone."

"Did she have any enemies? Anyone who might have wanted to harm her?" I asked, feeling the familiar grip of determination tighten around my chest.

"Enemies? Why so?" she asked, her eyes taking on a faraway look. "But there are those in this city who would exploit a young woman's dreams for their own gain. Talent agents, impresarios, patrons with more money than scruples. It's a tangled web we weave, Signore, and sometimes innocence is the first casualty."

"Where can I find these people?" I pressed, my instincts sharpening like the blade of a stiletto.

"I do not know," she stated. "It is not knowledge I want to have."

She turned her back to me and returned to her class. I cast a last gaze around the large dance hall and the trimmed young women who focused on their practice, not even bothering to glance my way.

The air was thick with the scent of crushed dreams and forbidden desires as I found my way out of the Palazzo della Danza. The street outside did not offer any freshness, but at least the air was different.

"Luigi Ferro," a sultry voice purred in my ear, and I turned to find myself face-to-face with a vision in a figure-hugging outfit. Her eyes sparkled like dark jewels beneath the blonde fringe, and I could feel the heat of her breath against my cheek as she leaned in closer. "You were asking questions about Elena, weren't you?"

"Who are you?" I asked, trying to maintain my composure despite the intoxicating allure of her presence.

"Call me Isabella," she replied, running a finger along the lapel of my jacket. "I may have some information for you..."

"Speak," I demanded as I fought to resist the temptation that seemed to coil seductively around my senses.

"Not here," she whispered. "Meet me at the Bar Vecchio Ponte at eight tonight."

She was gone as quickly as she had appeared. I followed her lithe figure as she danced her way back into the building.

*

I made my way through the maze of narrow streets to the address for Elena's apartment in the working-class district of Marghera. The worn building had seen better days, with peeling paint and rickety shutters. Inside, the musty hallway was dimly lit by bare bulbs. I climbed three flights of creaky stairs before arriving at her door.

When I knocked, the door swung open. A young woman with a mane of curly black hair peered out suspiciously.

"Who are you?" she inquired, her Italian tinged with a playful accent.

Introducing myself as a friend searching for Elena, I watched her face light up with a mix of recognition and something more enigmatic.

"I'm here about her disappearance," I said. "And you are...?"

"Giulia," she purred, her gaze lingering on me a moment too long before she swung the door open wider with a flourish. "Elena's roommate."

As I stepped into the cluttered apartment, Giulia's movements were fluid, almost dance-like. The small living area was a chaotic blend of a faded sofa, mismatched chairs, and a floor littered with dance paraphernalia.

"Excuse our little creative chaos," Giulia chuckled, her voice dripping with an allure that seemed to wrap around the clutter. "Elena, she's the organized one."

She said 'is', not 'was'. A flicker of hope or a slip of the tongue?

Offering me a glass of water, Giulia leaned in closer than necessary, her scent mingling with the room's bohemian aroma. As she spoke of Elena, her words painted a picture of a young woman drunk on Venice's artistic freedoms - nights filled with dance, poetry, and impromptu gatherings.

"Elena sought something... deeper," Giulia mused, her eyes holding mine. "A passion that her village couldn't offer. But she was frightened those last few days before she disappeared."

My heart raced. "Frightened of what?"

Giulia's glance darted around the room, her voice dropping to a whisper. "She got tangled up with some unsavory characters. Artists, promoters... She didn't know who to trust."

Leaning in closer, Giulia's breath brushed against my ear, her words a silken thread weaving a web. "It's a dangerous game, this world of art and shadows," she murmured, her lips barely an inch from mine. Her hand found its way to my arm, her touch light but charged with an unspoken promise.

The room seemed to constrict around us, the air thick with an electric tension. Her eyes, deep pools of mystery, locked onto mine, challenging me, pulling me deeper into her ensnaring gaze. I was acutely conscious of the peril, of her seductive allure clouding my focus, yet a part of me yearned to yield to the temptation.

Then, in a bold move, Giulia closed the gap between us, her lips meeting mine in a kiss that was both a promise and a distraction. Her hand, now boldly caressing my thigh, was a whisper of danger and desire, blurring the lines between professional resolve and the human pull of attraction.

With a surge of strength, I pulled away from the young woman's alluring lips, grabbing her shoulders and gently pushing her away.

Her slim, shapely leg snaked around mine, and the soft fabric of her sheer blouse hung loosely over her bare bosom, the pink, firm nipples doing their best to pierce the fabric. I blinked and rose, swallowed hard, and thanked Giulia for her information.

"Here's my number if you think of anything else," I said. Giulia took it hesitantly and slipped it down between her pert breasts. She threw me a seductive smile, winked, and slipped inside. Darkness was falling, cloaking Venice in mystery. And somewhere, hidden beneath its veil, was Elena.

Elena had stumbled into something dangerous, but was Giulia a beacon of truth or another layer of deception in this Venetian mystery? I needed to navigate this seductive maze with caution.

I left the apartment with an unsettled feeling. Things were not as they seemed in this decaying neighborhood on Venice's fringe. Elena had gotten caught up in something dangerous. But I was determined to find out what.

The night air in Venice carried whispers of secrets and sin, the scent of saltwater mingling with the perfume of temptation. I navigated the dimly lit streets, searching for the bar where the dancer had promised to meet me.

I passed over the Rialto Bridge as I reviewed the facts. Elena Popescu, a young dancer full of hopes and dreams, vanished two weeks ago without a trace. The local cops wrote it off as just another runaway chasing fame in the big city. But her father wasn't convinced, and neither was I. Her dance instructor had praised her dancing but had not wanted to explain further. And Elena's roommate Giulia had been more keen to explore my body than talking about her girlfriend.

I found the bar nestled in a narrow alley off the Grand Canal. Bar Vecchio Ponte was a sanctuary for the city's artists, a place where creativity and coffee were always brewing. The moment I stepped inside, the world transformed. The aroma of rich espresso brewed to perfection hung in the air, mingling with the sharp tang of red wine that had kissed many an artist's lips. The walls, a canvas of history, were adorned with sketches and paintings, each telling its own story.

At one table, a group of poets animatedly debated the virtues of modernism versus classicism, their passionate gestures punctuating the smoky air. Nearby, a painter, her fingers stained with vibrant hues, shared a laugh with a sculptor whose clay-speckled apron told of a day's hard work.

The gentle strumming of a guitar added a melodious backdrop to the cacophony of conversations. It was played by an old musician whose eyes had seen the changing tides of art, his fingers dancing over the strings with the grace of a seasoned storyteller.

In a dimly lit corner, a young playwright scribbled fervently in a worn notebook, occasionally pausing to sip from a mug of steaming coffee, her gaze lost in a world of her own making.

The scent of oil paint and turpentine wafted from a canvas propped against the bar, where an artist with a beret lost himself in his latest masterpiece, oblivious to the buzz around him.

Each person in Bar Vecchio Ponte was a thread in the vibrant tapestry of Venice's artistic tapestry, their laughter, debates, and the clinking of glasses creating a symphony that celebrated art in all its forms. In this haven, creativity wasn't just present; it was alive, pulsating with the heartbeat of the city's soul.

I found a place at the bar and ordered a glass of gin with a twist of lime.

"Ah, Signor Ferro," Isabella purred, her crimson gown rippling like molten lava as she moved up beside me. Men all over the bar followed her every move, savoring every graceful curve. Her blonde curls flowed freely over her slender shoulders. The red lips smiled up at me.

"Ah, Signorina," I raised an eyebrow, intrigued by this beautiful encounter. "You wanted to talk."

The dancer's gaze flickered with recognition, a hint of fear flashing beneath the surface. "Why do you want to know about her?" she asked cautiously, her voice low and husky.

"Let's just say a friend is worried about her," I replied, leaning against a marble pillar, my eyes never leaving hers. "Elena disappeared some weeks ago, and I aim to find her."

"I knew Elena," the dancer admitted, biting her lip and glancing around nervously. "But I don't know what happened to her. There are...rumors."

"Rumors? About what?" I pressed, keeping my voice steady despite the tightening knot in my gut.

"Dark dealings, Signore. Unsavory characters preying on young artists like Elena." She hesitated, her eyes darting away from mine. "I shouldn't be talking to you. It's dangerous."

"Sometimes danger is the price we pay for truth," I countered, searching her face for any sign of wavering. "You could help me save her."

"Indeed," Isabella said, her smile sly as it played upon her full lips. "Perhaps I can shed some light on the darkness that surrounds you."

"Alright, bella," I replied, my interest piqued. "What do you know?"

"Venice's artistic community is no stranger to shadows," she began, her voice low and conspiratorial. "There are those who would do anything for power, wealth, or fame – even if it meant sacrificing their very soul."

"Go on," I urged, my patience wearing thin.

"A few weeks ago, a priceless painting was stolen from a private collection, and rumor has it that the thief was none other than an aspiring dancer – a young woman who matches Elena's description." Isabella paused, gauging my reaction. "It is said that the painting holds secrets, ones that could unravel the very fabric of our city's history."

"Secrets?" I asked my skepticism plain.

"Venice is built on more than just water and stone, Signor Ferro," she replied cryptically. "There are those who would kill for such knowledge."

I considered her words, the cogs in my mind turning as I weighed my options. A stolen painting, a missing dancer, and a city teeming with treachery – what was the connection? And how could I unravel this tangled web before it was too late?

"Who can I trust?" I whispered, the weight of my dilemma bearing down upon me like the oppressive heat of a Venetian summer's night.

"In this city, trust is a luxury few can afford. You must rely on your instincts – they have served you well thus far, have they not?"

"Very well, Isabella," I said finally, my resolve

hardening like steel. "Show me where to look, and perhaps we can shed some light on this missing painting and Elena's disappearance."

"Ah, Signor Ferro, if only it were that simple," she replied, her eyes gleaming with a mixture of amusement and pity. "The painting's whereabouts remain a mystery, but I can offer you a starting point."

"Which is?"

"An artist by the name of Matteo Romano," she answered, her voice barely above a whisper. "He may not have the answers you seek, but he knows the undercurrents of this city better than most. Find him, and perhaps you'll find the truth you so desperately desire. Elena modeled for him."

"Can I have your number if I have further questions?" I asked, pulling up my cell.

"This is not a date, Signore," she smiled, shaking her head. "You know where to find me if I want to be found…"

*

I headed back towards the hotel, my mind churning over the day's revelations. Venice's glossy veneer concealed a rotten core - Elena stumbled into its grasp, but why?

Lost in thought, I barely noticed the footsteps echoing behind me on the empty street. A prickle on my neck snapped me alert just as a figure lunged from the shadows.

I spun, deflecting the blow. My attacker was a wiry

young man with desperation in his eyes. We grappled, then broke apart, circling each other.

"Why are you following me?" I demanded.

"You're asking dangerous questions," he spat back. "Leave Venice if you value your life."

I stood firm. "Not until I find out what happened to Elena."

With a guttural cry, he came at me again. I sidestepped his charge, seizing his arm and using his momentum to hurl him against the brick wall. He slumped down, dazed.

I pressed my foot on his chest. "You tried to warn me off. Who sent you?"

He grimaced in pain. "Can't say. But you won't like what you find."

I heard a noise and glanced up. Two men emerged from the shadows. My informant took the chance to scuttle away.

The men approached. "Luigi Ferro? You need to come with us." One cracked his knuckles.

My muscles tensed. I was outnumbered but wouldn't go quietly. "I think I'll pass," I said. Then I struck.

I drove my fist into the first man's solar plexus, doubling him over. As he gasped for breath, I grabbed his head and slammed my knee up into his face. He crumpled to the ground.

The second man pulled a knife and slashed at me. I leapt back, the blade hissing past my chest. We circled each other warily.

He feinted left, then stabbed right. I seized his wrist,

stopping the blade inches from my gut. We strained against each other, muscles trembling.

With a burst of effort, I wrenched his arm down and smashed my elbow into his face. He reeled back with a cry, dropping the knife. I scooped it up and leveled it at him.

"Now, you're going to tell me who sent you, or our next dance will end less pleasantly."

He spat blood. "Go to hell."

I shrugged. "Have it your way." I flipped the knife and clubbed him across the temple with the hilt. He collapsed unconscious.

I rifled through their pockets but found nothing to identify them. Sirens wailed in the distance. Time to disappear.

As I slipped into the shadows, my mind raced. Someone clearly wanted me gone, which meant I was getting close. I had to find Elena before they silenced us both for good.

3

The morning broke with a soft mist rolling in from the Adriatic, wrapping the canals and footpaths in a gauzy haze. I sat at the hotel's breakfast bar, nursing a strong cappuccino, poring over information on cases of stolen artwork. Venice, with its mysterious charm, seemed to weave its secrets into the very air. It was a city adept at hiding its truths, and this case was proving to be a labyrinth of its own.

My phone vibrated with another message from Caterina, my sometimes girlfriend, suggesting dinner tonight. I set the phone aside; my mind was deep in the enigma of Elena Popescu now.

Leaving the hotel, I walked through the narrow, winding streets of Venice, the air rich with the smell of murky water and cheap perfume. I was heading towards the address I had found for Matteo Romano. His artist's studio was hidden in an old palazzo; its once grand facade was now a mask of peeling paint and rusted shutters.

I knocked twice before pushing the door open. The studio welcomed me with the heady smell of oil paint and turpentine. Romano was there, brush in hand, standing beside an easel. He turned to me with a look of disdain, his eyes as enigmatic as the city itself.

"What do you want?" he barked, taking the cigarette from his lips.

I nodded in greeting, stepping inside and glancing

around at the half-finished canvases stacked against the walls.

"Elena Popescu," I clarified, watching Romano's expression change to one of confusion.

"I don't know no one by that name," he said, setting down his brush. "And I've never heard of such a strange name."

A chill ran down my spine at the denial; it didn't sit right with him. Something was off here. "You sure about that? That's strange. Because she was one of your models, no?"

Matteo clenched his jaw. "Models come and go. I don't keep track."

"Right. Especially when they discover you're forging Old Masters in between sessions."

Matteo paled. I had him.

"That's nonsense," he sputtered. "Slander! I only work with what I'm given, Signore."

But there was something in the way he shifted his gaze away, something in the way he avoided eye contact. I couldn't quite put my finger on it, but I felt like I was missing something important.

"Why are you here?" Romano asked, changing the subject abruptly.

"Maybe just the same as you," I replied, eyeing a partially completed portrait of a woman with long, wavy brown hair that reminded me of Elena Popescu. "I'm chasing after a ghost."

"A beautiful ghost, I hope?" The artist smirked, turning towards me. There was a hint of mischief in his eyes now, as if he knew something more than he was letting on.

I took a step closer, drawn in by the allure of whatever secrets Romano might be keeping. "You know, there are always whispers in this city. Secrets that can't stay buried for long. But, if Signorina Popescu's name is unknown, you may know of some art forgery."

"I know nothing of such things, Signore," he replied, flicking ash on the floor.

"Save it. Elena's gone missing, and it's connected to your...extracurricular activities. The kind that runs through Venice's underbelly."

Matteo's eyes darted around the studio. He lowered his voice. "Even if that were true, I'd have no part in anything unsavory. I'm just a simple artist making ends meet."

I stepped even closer, trapping him against the easel.

"A simple artist who knows more than he lets on. Your secrets are coming out, Matteo. Like blood seeping through a bandage. Tell me what you know about Elena and Venice before it's too late."

Matteo trembled, grasping the easel for support. When he spoke, his voice was a hoarse whisper.

"I've already said too much, Signore. Now, please, let me work in peace."

I studied his face - the fear in his eyes betraying the truth. With a last stream of smoke between us, I turned and left. The game was on.

My phone buzzed in my pocket - an unwelcome interruption. I excused myself and answered the call, feeling Romano's eyes on me as I stepped away.

"Luigi?" came the voice of Elena's roommate, Giulia. "I found something you might want to see. I found it while tidying our flat. I think it could be important."

"Where are you now?" I asked, glancing back at Romano, who had returned to his work, feigning disinterest in my conversation.

"Still at the flat," she replied. "Can you come over?"

"Give me twenty minutes," I said, hanging up and slipping my phone back into my pocket. I turned to Romano, who was watching me with an unreadable expression. "It seems I have other business to attend to."

"Of course, Signore," he said, nodding curtly as I took my leave.

The sun was almost at its zenith as I arrived at Giulia and Elena's flat, casting short shadows across the narrow streets. I rang the doorbell, and as the door swung open, Giulia greeted me with a sly smile.

"Hello, Luigi," she purred, her dark eyes sparkling with mischief. She wore a sheer black robe that left little to the imagination, and the scent of jasmine filled the air.

"Giulia," I replied, trying to remain focused. "What have you found?"

"Ah, yes," she said, stepping aside to let me in. "But first, let me pour you a drink."

"Giulia, it is barely noon. I need to know what you've found," I insisted, my patience wearing thin.

"Very well," she sighed, leading me to the living room. "But you're missing out on some fine Italian wine."

As I followed her through the dimly lit flat, I couldn't

help but be drawn in by the curve of her hips and the way the robe clung to her body. She was tempting, no doubt about it, and I felt the familiar stirrings of desire within me.

The flat was still a mess, strewn with clothes and half-empty bottles of wine.

"Are you sure you don't want that drink?" she asked, her voice low and sultry.

"Giulia, don't..."

"Please, Mr. Ferro. Just one drink. We can talk about Elena afterward."

"Maybe just one," I conceded, feeling the pull of temptation beginning to overpower reason.

"Good choice," she whispered, her breath hot against my ear as she led me back to the kitchen. And even though I knew better, I allowed myself to be swept up in the seduction and secrecy of the Venetian ambiance.

"Over there," she said, gesturing to a small table in the corner. "I found that note."

As I reached for the note, Giulia slowly approached me, her body pressed against mine. I could feel her warm breath on my neck, igniting a fire within me.

"Leave it for now," she whispered, her fingers deftly working the buttons of my shirt.

Our surroundings faded away as she locked her amber eyes onto mine, filled with an insatiable desire. The air was thick with anticipation as we explored each other's bodies, giving into the unspoken tension that had been building between us.

I knew full well I was being seduced, but at that moment, all thoughts of Elena and the case vanished like smoke in the wind. Giulia's black robe fell to her feet, revealing a stunning young body. We couldn't resist any longer, succumbing to our primal urges as we made passionate love on the cold, hard floor. Nothing else mattered at that moment except the intense connection between us.

"Salute," she whispered, raising her glass in a toast as we came back to reality.

"Salute," I gasped. Our glasses clinked, and we drank in silence, the cool, soothing sweetness mixed with temptation.

When our glasses were empty, Giulia took my hand and led me back to the table. The note lay there, forgotten for now, as she pressed her body against mine.

"Luigi," she breathed against my neck. "You should know... I found the note by Elena's bed. I think it might help you find her."

I hesitated for a moment before looking at it. My eyes scanned the words and numbers scribbled in haste, excitement building as I realized the potential significance of the information.

"Giulia, this could be the lead I need," I muttered, tucking the note into my pocket. "I have to follow this up."

"Of course," she murmured, her lips brushing against mine one last time before stepping back. "Just promise me you'll be careful."

"I will," I assured her, buttoning up my shirt and grabbing my jacket. As I left the flat, I couldn't shake the feeling that Giulia had given me more than just a valuable clue; she'd given me a taste of the allure that seemed to surround Elena's disappearance.

I clutched the note in my hand, feeling the weight and significance of the hastily scribbled digits on the crumpled paper. My heart pounded like a relentless drumbeat as I dialed the phone number on the note, my fingers trembling with anticipation. It rang once, twice, and then a gruff voice answered on the other end.

"Pronto?" a man barked.

"Who is this?" I demanded, my voice steady despite the uncertainty gnawing at my insides.

"Who's asking?" came the curt reply.

"My name is Ferro. I'm looking for information about Elena Popescu."

There was a pause, and then the man chuckled darkly.

"Good luck with that," he sneered, and the line went dead.

The phone number on the note pointed to Rimini.

"Rimini," I muttered under my breath, my voice barely audible above the distant hum of the canal waters. Elena's last known whereabouts, the city where her dreams of stardom may have led her, and now – it seemed – the epicenter of this twisted web of forgery and deceit.

I raised the note to my face, inhaling deeply, searching for any lingering traces of her scent. Instead, all I found was the faint aroma of Giulia's perfume, a heady mix of jasmine and vanilla that still clung to my clothes from our brief encounter. The memory of her touch sent a shiver down my spine, and I cursed myself for allowing desire to cloud my judgment.

"Focus, Ferro," I admonished myself, shaking my head as if to dispel the lingering haze of temptation. This was no time for distractions; Elena's fate hung in the balance, and I was her only hope.

*

Rimini unfolded before me like a siren's song, its sleek and sophisticated essence wrapping itself around me, tightening like a corset. The city breathed temptation with every sultry exhale, her seductive whispers promising decadent secrets waiting to be uncovered. I stepped out of the train station and strolled towards the waterfront, my eyes scanning the throngs of sun-kissed tourists and elegant locals as they reveled in the heady cocktail of power and desire that seemed to fuel this playground of the rich and infamous.

"Ferro!" a voice called out, cutting through the symphony of laughter and idle chatter.

Turning, I came face to face with Commissario Gastone Carlotto, a man known for his skepticism towards private investigators like me. His crisp, bespoke suits with perfectly pressed creases and fine Italian stitching stood out among the sea of t-shirts and jeans. Hailing from Milan, he knew how to dress and enjoyed it.

"Ferro," Carlotto repeated, his tone carrying the formal air of a man who took his role at the Italian crime squad seriously. His eyes, sharp and assessing, seemed to take in every detail.

"We need to talk," he said, his voice carrying an authoritative edge.

I raised an eyebrow, curious. "About?"

Carlotto's gaze was steady, his expression giving nothing away. "It's about a phone call you made. To a number in Rimini."

A slight tension crept into my muscles. That call was a pivotal lead in my search for Elena, and now it appeared to be part of something larger.

"What about it?" I asked, striving to keep my voice even.

"The number you called is under our surveillance," Carlotto revealed in a whisper, his eyes never leaving mine. "We've been monitoring it as part of an ongoing investigation."

Surprise and a hint of irritation washed over me. The number was a crucial link to Elena, and now it was ensnared in a broader, possibly more perilous situation.

"And why is this of concern to me, Commissario?" I inquired, keeping my composure.

"Because, Ferro, whoever you're looking for might be caught up in something much bigger than a missing person's case," Carlotto replied. His tone was stern, a reminder of the gravity of the situation.

I absorbed this information, my mind already racing with the implications. If the police monitored that number, it suggested that Elena's situation was entangled in a complex web I had yet to fully understand.

"Can you share anything about this investigation?" I asked, hoping for any detail that could aid my search.

Carlotto shook his head, his expression unyielding. "You know I can't disclose specifics, Ferro. But I advise caution. You're entering dangerous territory."

His warning sent a shiver through me. I had always navigated within the law's boundaries, but this case was personal, complicated further by this new revelation.

"Thanks for the warning, Commissario," I responded, already pondering my next steps. "I'll be careful."

Carlotto studied me for a moment longer as if deciding whether to add more, then nodded sharply and turned away, his figure receding into the vibrant street scene.

Left alone, I stood pondering the new layer of complexity added to the case. The intercepted call meant I had to tread carefully, but retreat wasn't an option. Elena's safety, and possibly that of others, hinged on my actions. I inhaled deeply, steeling myself for the intricate web of intrigue that lay ahead. This was more than a mere investigation; it was a journey into a labyrinth of shadows, and I was determined to uncover the truth, no matter how convoluted the path.

I walked along the seaside streets of Rimini, surrounded by modern hotels and restaurants that bore silent witness to countless stories. The air was heavy with the scent of fresh seafood and strong espresso, mingling with the distant echoes of laughter and music from the nearby establishments. I could feel the city's pulse beneath my feet, a rhythm as old as time itself.

My walk was not for stretching my legs or clearing my thoughts; it had a purpose. I aimed for an underground club. I turned down a side street and stopped before a nondescript door, barely visible in the shadows.

Behind that door was one of the many secrets of Rimini – a haven for criminals and those who profit from their illicit dealings, always one step ahead of the law. Elena may have unwittingly stumbled upon their operations, or perhaps she was lured into their web by the promise of fame and fortune. Either way, this was a good place to start.

My heart was pounding with the thrill of the chase. For better or worse, the die was cast, and only fate would determine the outcome.

The room was dimly lit, shadows dancing on the walls as the flickering light cast a surreal glow over the scattered papers and photographs strewn across the table. My fingers itched to explore the evidence before me, every fiber of my being yearning for the truth that lay hidden within their folds.

I took a deep breath, steeling myself for what lay ahead. With each step I took into the shadowy den, I felt myself sinking deeper into a world of forbidden desires and whispered promises – a realm where beauty and sin coexisted in perfect harmony.

"Buonasera, Signore," purred a sultry voice as a woman with raven locks and eyes that burned as embers approached me. She wore a dress as red as the neon sign outside, her curves accentuated by the tight fabric. "Looking for some company tonight?"

"Perhaps," I replied, taking a sip of my gin with a twist of lime. "But first, I have some questions."

"Ah, an inquisitive man," she mused, her lips curving into a seductive smile. "I do love a good mystery."

"Then perhaps you can help me solve one," I said, my tone as smooth as the finest silk. "I'm looking for information on certain... establishments in the area. Ones offering young ladies as dancers, entertainers, or something more... intimate."

Her eyes narrowed, the fire within them flickering dangerously. "A dangerous game you're playing, Signore. Some secrets are best left in the shadows."

"Unfortunately for me, I've never been one to shy away from danger," I confessed, my heart pounding with a mixture of adrenaline and desire. "And when it comes to finding the truth, no secret is safe."

"Very well," she acquiesced, her voice barely above a whisper. "There are several places you might find what you seek. But be warned – the men who control these establishments are not to be trifled with. Cross them, and you may find yourself on the wrong side of a knife."

"Are you speaking from personal experience?" I asked, a note of concern creeping into my voice.

"Let's just say I've seen enough to know that some doors should remain closed," she replied cryptically before turning on her heel and disappearing into the shadows.

As I jotted down the names and locations provided by the mysterious woman, I couldn't help but feel a sense of foreboding. With each new lead, I was venturing further into unknown territory – a place where darkness reigned supreme, and the line between friend and foe was as blurred as the ink on my notepad.

But as I looked around at the faces lost in their own private fantasies – the men and women who had willingly surrendered themselves to temptation's siren call – I knew that there was no turning back now. For in the labyrinthine depths of Rimini's underworld, I would find not only the answers I sought but also the key to unlocking the chains that bound us all.

The sultry perfume of lust hung heavily in the air as I made my way further inside the dimly lit establishment. Velvet curtains draped over every curve, casting shadows that danced with an almost lascivious intent, and the seductive melody of a jazz crooner filled the room like a lover's whisper.

"Luigi! My old friend!" The voice was warm, its familiarity cutting through the haze like a knife. I turned to see Guido, the proprietor of this den of temptation. His face bore the lines of a life lived on the edge of society, his eyes twinkling with a roguish charm that had served him well in matters of both business and pleasure.

"Guido," I replied, clasping his outstretched hand firmly. "It's been a while."

"Too long, my friend," he said, his smile revealing teeth that were as sharp as his wit. "What brings you to my humble abode?"

"Business, unfortunately," I replied, allowing myself a small smile. "I'm looking for someone."

"Ah, aren't we all?" Guido chuckled his laughter, a low rumble that seemed to echo throughout the room. "Well, come. Let us drink, and perhaps your quarry will reveal herself."

As we sipped our gin, the twist of lime accentuating its bittersweet flavor, I found myself drawn into the intoxicating world that Guido had created. Each woman who passed before me was a living, breathing work of art – their bodies adorned with nothing more than the finest silk and lace, their smiles promising pleasures beyond even the wildest imagination.

But as much as I longed to lose myself in their embrace, I knew that I could not afford to succumb to distraction. And none of them was Elena Popescu.

"Guido," I said finally, my voice barely audible above the sultry beat of the music. "I must go."

"Very well," he replied, his gaze never leaving the dancers who swayed to the rhythm of his world. "But remember, Luigi – the door is always open."

As I made my way back into the evening, the lingering scent of temptation still clinging to my skin, I couldn't help but feel the weight of the shadows that surrounded me. Each step brought with it a new sense of foreboding as if I were being followed by something unseen yet undeniably present.

And as I paused beneath the cold glow of a streetlight, its harsh glare casting my silhouette against the pavement, I reflected on the risks and dangers ahead. This treacherous path would lead me not only to the truth but also to the very heart of darkness itself.

Unbeknownst to me, a shadow loomed behind, watching my every move with an inscrutable intent. The game was afoot, and it was clear that I was no longer alone in this deadly dance of deception.

The morning sun cast a warm glow over the streets of Rimini, reflecting off the ancient Roman ruins as I cruised along on my Vespa. The air was thick with the scent of freshly baked bread and strong espresso, the kind that could jolt even the most hardened detective back to life. I had spent the night at home, and Caterina's cute face still lingered in my thoughts like the aftertaste of last night's gin; I reminded myself that I had work to do.

The list of locations I had scribbled down last night was in my pocket. The first address on my list was an agency tucked away in a narrow alley, its entrance guarded by a pair of velvet curtains that seemed to whisper secrets about the people who had come and gone through them. I parked my Vespa nearby and adjusted my jacket before stepping inside.

"Buongiorno," I greeted the staff, my eyes scanning the room for any sign of Elena Popescu or her tormentor, the Agent. The dimly lit space was filled with the murmur of hushed conversations, and sultry music played softly in the background.

"Can I help you?" A woman behind the reception desk asked, her red lips curving into a polite smile that didn't quite reach her eyes.

"My name is Luigi Ferro," I introduced myself, my voice firm but courteous. "I'm looking for information about a young dancer." I pulled out a photograph of

Elena from my pocket and slid it across the counter. "She's been caught up in some trouble, and I wonder if she has passed through your agency."

The woman glanced at the photo, her expression carefully neutral.

"I'm afraid we don't know anything about this girl," she replied, her fingers drumming an anxious rhythm on the countertop.

"Really?" I pressed, feeling the familiar itch of suspicion beneath my collar. "Because I have reason to believe that your agency is involved in exploiting young artists like Elena."

"Signore," the woman said, her voice trembling ever so slightly, "our agency is a legitimate business. We help talented dancers find work, nothing more."

"Is that so?" I leaned in closer, my eyes narrowing into cold, unyielding daggers. I made a decision to modify the truth a bit. "Then why is it that multiple girls from your agency have come forward, detailing how you coerce them into performing lewd strip-tease acts?"

The woman's facade of confidence wavers, her voice trembling as she struggles to find an excuse.

"I–I can explain," she stammered, her words laced with desperation. "We offered Elena a chance at fame and fortune as a professional dancer, but she was too weak to accept."

My grip on the table tightens, my knuckles turning white at her blatant lies.

"Interesting," I growled, filing away the information. So Elena had resisted the lure of easy money, choosing to stay true to her passion for dance rather than selling her soul to the highest bidder. That kind of determination wouldn't go unnoticed by those who preyed on innocence.

"Thank you for your time," I said, pocketing the photograph and preparing to leave. But before I could make my exit, the woman spoke up again.

"Signore, please be careful," she warned, her eyes darting nervously around the room. "There are powerful people involved in this business, and they won't take kindly to anyone poking their nose where it doesn't belong."

"Trust me, signora," I replied with a wry smile. "I'm no stranger to danger."

And with that, I stepped back out into the sunlight, the weight of the woman's words settling heavily on my shoulders as I continued my hunt for the truth.

The day was growing hotter as I made my way to the next agency on my list. The clamor of people going about their daily business filled the air with a sense of urgency. My thoughts were consumed by the image of Elena Popescu, her innocence and determination in stark contrast to the city's dark underbelly. I had to find her.

As I entered the second agency, a shiver ran down my spine as if an icy finger had caressed the back of my neck. A tall, thin woman with a pallid complexion stood behind the reception desk, her hollow eyes betraying a mixture of fear and suspicion. Her gaze followed me like a caged bird, unable to escape its confines but aware of the predator lurking just beyond.

"Good morning, Signorina," I ventured, offering a friendly smile that felt out of place in the oppressive atmosphere. "I'm here to inquire about someone who may have crossed paths with your agency."

"Who might that be?" she asked, her voice barely more than a whisper. I could hear the quiver in her tone, which only served to heighten the unease that seemed to permeate the room.

"Her name is Elena Popescu," I replied, producing the photograph I had shown at the previous agency. The woman's eyes widened in recognition, and her hands began to tremble ever so slightly.

"Ah... yes," she stammered, her gaze darting nervously between the photograph and my face. "Elena was... involved with our agency for a short time."

"Can you tell me what happened to her?" I pressed, the scent of her fear spurring me on like a bloodhound on the trail of its quarry.

"Signor..." she hesitated, swallowing hard before continuing. "Elena was... removed by some associates of the Agent after she refused to participate in a pornographic film."

"Removed?" I echoed, my grip on the photograph tightening until my knuckles turned white. "Where did they take her?"

"I... I don't know," she confessed, terror etched into every line of her face. "But if you're looking for Elena, you should be very careful. The people who took her are dangerous."

"Signorina, I've spent my life dealing with dangerous people," I replied softly, feeling a sudden kinship with this frightened creature before me. "And I won't rest until I find out what happened to Elena."

"Please, Signore," she pleaded, her voice cracking under the strain of her emotions. "Don't let them hurt you, too."

"Trust me," I reassured her, pocketing the photograph and turning to leave. "I have no intention of becoming their prey."

As I stepped back out, onto the sun-drenched streets of Rimini, I couldn't help but feel an icy chill settling in the pit of my stomach. The beautiful facade of the city hid a darkness that threatened to consume all who dared to challenge it. But I had made a promise to myself and to Elena Popescu: I would expose the truth, no matter the cost.

The sultry wind grazed my cheeks as I left the agency, the truth about Elena weighing heavily on my mind. The afternoon sun cast cooling shadows across the narrow streets of Rimini, the contrast of light and dark mirroring the city's dual nature. I couldn't help but feel like I was being watched, a sensation that had nagged at me since I began my investigation.

"Signor Ferro," a voice hissed from behind, heavy with malice. I turned to face the speaker, but the alleyway was shrouded in darkness. The shadows seemed alive, pulsating with sinister intent. My hand instinctively reached for the gun hidden beneath my tailored jacket.

"Who's there?" I demanded, my eyes scanning the gloom for movement. The tension in the air crackled like electricity, the atmosphere thick with the scent of danger.

"Ah, Signor Ferro," the same venomous voice taunted, emerging from the blackness. "I hope you're not too uncomfortable."

"Who are you?" I snarled, my anger momentarily overpowering the fear coursing through my body. "And what do you want with me?"

"Names are irrelevant," the voice replied dismissively. "As for what I want...well, that's simple. Your investigation into Elena ends here. Permanently."

"Or what?" I spat, defiance surging through my veins. "You'll kill me? That won't stop others from asking questions."

"Perhaps not," the voice conceded, a malicious smile evident in its tone. "But it will serve as a warning to anyone foolish enough to meddle in our affairs. You may think yourself clever, Signor Ferro, but there are forces at play far beyond your comprehension."

"I've dealt with worse than you before," I growled, my hands clenched into fists of pure determination. "And I'll do it again. For Elena and for all the girls like her who've fallen prey to this city's dark underbelly."

"Very well," the voice responded coolly, retreating back into the shadows. "Let the games begin."

I barely had time to react before a crushing blow connected with my skull, sending me spiraling into unconsciousness.

*

When I finally awakened, groggy and disoriented, I found myself in a dimly lit room, the walls closing in around me like a suffocating embrace. My head throbbed with pain, and I could taste iron on my tongue – blood. I'd been overpowered and taken against my will, which only fueled my determination to uncover the truth.

"Where am I?" I muttered, struggling to sit up, my muscles screaming in protest. The darkness around me was oppressive, broken only by the faint glow of a single candle flickering in the corner. It was impossible to discern any details of my surroundings.

The pain that throbbed through my skull was a cruel reminder of the shadowy figure's parting words. I struggled to sit up, the dim light from a solitary naked bulb doing little to illuminate my surroundings. The room seemed to close in around me like a fist, suffocating and oppressive. My thoughts whirled, but I couldn't afford to dwell on them for long. Elena was out there somewhere, and time was running out.

As if summoned by my determination, the door creaked open, revealing a vision of red-haired beauty framed against the darkness. Isabella – the Venetian dancer I'd encountered earlier in my investigation – stepped into the room, her eyes filled with concern.

"Signor Ferro," she murmured, her voice as rich and sultry as a sip of Amarone. "I heard about your investigation and thought you might need some help."

"Isabella," I breathed, relief washing over me like waves lapping at the shores of the Adriatic. "How did you find me?"

"News flies on swift wings in this city," she responded, her voice laced with a hint of mystery as she deftly tucked a rogue strand of auburn hair behind her ear. "Especially about a dashing outsider who's stirring the pot with perilous inquiries." Her gaze held mine, intense and knowing. "I called your office, you see. Caterina was quite chatty – mentioned you were in Rimini, following a trail of addresses. A list she seemed to know by heart."

"Hmm," I grunted with a mix of gratitude and surprise. "Someone should have warned me about the perils of curiosity," I muttered, half-smiling despite the pain.

"Perhaps they should," Isabella agreed, her eyes twinkling with mischief. "But then we wouldn't be sharing this intimate moment, would we?"

Intimate wasn't exactly how I'd have described our current predicament, but there was no denying this dancer's beauty. The firelight danced across her porcelain skin, casting shadows that only accentuated her exquisite features.

"Enough with the pleasantries," I said, forcing myself to focus on the task at hand. "What do you know about Elena?"

"Patience, Signor Ferro," she admonished gently, her fingers brushing against my cheek in a feather-light caress. "All will be revealed in due time."

"Time is a luxury we don't have, Isabella," I insisted, my voice raw with urgency. "Tell me what you know."

"Very well," she sighed, the warmth of her breath tickling my neck as she leaned in closer. "I've heard whispers of a secretive auction where girls like Elena are sold to the highest bidder – most often to sex traffickers."

"Where?" I demanded, my heart pounding like the relentless beat of a techno track.

"An abandoned warehouse on the outskirts of the city," she replied, her gaze never leaving mine. "But it's heavily guarded, and only those with invitations can enter."

"Then it looks like we'll need an invitation," I said grimly, determination surging through me like a jolt of espresso.

"Indeed," Isabella murmured, her lips curving into a seductive smile. "But first, let's get you out of this dreary place. You're in no condition for heroics just yet."

"Your concern is touching," I retorted, but she was right. My body still ached from the earlier encounter, and I'd need all my strength for the challenges that lay ahead.

"Sometimes, even the hardest hearts need a little tender care," she whispered, helping me to my feet. "And I'm more than willing to provide it."

As we left the dimly lit room behind us, I couldn't help but feel that our alliance was both a blessing and a curse. The allure of Isabella's beauty threatened to distract me from my mission, and yet her knowledge of Rimini's dark underbelly would prove invaluable in the search for Elena. Desire and duty entwined like the sinuous limbs of tango, but I'd dance that dance for as long as it took to bring Elena home.

The sun dipped low in the sky, casting long shadows

on the ancient cobblestone streets of Rimini. Isabella and I huddled together at a corner café, our heads bent close as we plotted our next move. The aroma of freshly brewed coffee mingled with the faint scent of her perfume, intoxicating me like some potent elixir.

"Alright," I said, taking a slow sip of my gin and tonic, savoring the sharp bite of the alcohol and the tang of lime. "We need to find a way into this auction. Any ideas?"

Isabella leaned in closer, her dark eyes gleaming with determination. "We'll pose as bidders," she whispered, her warm breath brushing against my ear. "I have connections. I can get us an invitation."

"Are you sure?" I asked, my suspicions momentarily flaring. This beautiful dancer seemed almost too eager to help me, and I had to remind myself where my loyalties lay.

"Trust me," she purred, her fingers lightly tracing patterns on the back of my hand. "I've been navigating these treacherous waters for years. I know how to make people… believe. You'll be the wealthy, sleazy buyer, and I'll be the slutty girl at your side." She smiled at me and threw back her hair.

"Very well," I acquiesced, my pulse quickening under her touch. "What do we need to do?"

"I need to dash off to the Rimini Outlets and get myself a slutty short and terribly expensive outfit," she said, rising gracefully from her seat. "You, just be prepared to play your part. Can you do that, Ferro?"

"Of course," I replied, trying to sound more confident than I felt. "I'm nothing if not adaptable."

"Good," she murmured, pressing her lips to my cheek in a lingering kiss. "Meet me tomorrow night, and we'll put our plan into action."

As Isabella vanished into the twilight, I pulled out my phone, knowing there was one more person I needed to inform about the auction. Dialing the number, I waited for Commissario Carlotto to pick up.

"Carlotto," he barked, his gruff voice a stark contrast to Isabella's sultry tones.

"Commissario, it's Ferro. I've got some information about Elena Popescu," I said, my words clipped and businesslike.

"Go on," he urged, clearly intrigued.

"Isabella, a dancer I met in Venice, informed me of an auction tomorrow night. Elena will be sold to the highest bidder and–"

"Luigi," Carlotto cut me off. "This is risky business you're getting into."

"Desperate times, Commissario," I replied, tugging at the cuffs of my tailored suit. "We need to find Elena before it's too late."

"Agreed." Carlotto nodded solemnly. "What do you have in mind?"

"Isabella and I will infiltrate the auction as bidders, blend in with the crowd, and gather intel. We'll need your help with equipment and backup."

"I'll see what I can do," he said, ending the call.

5

The Lambo roared as I pushed the pedal, its engine a hellish symphony announcing our arrival. Isabella rode shotgun, legs stretched out and her hair wild from the wind. A friend had lent me the beast of a machine – a temporary upgrade from my trusty Vespa – and I must admit, the adrenaline coursing through me was intoxicating. I couldn't help but grin as we pulled up to the auction venue, the sleek black Lamborghini cutting an imposing figure amidst the sea of more discrete luxury vehicles.

"Ready for some chaos, bella?" I asked, glancing at Isabella before stepping out onto the pavement.

"I believe so, Ferro," she replied with a wicked smile. Commissario Carlotto had set us up with two-way radio earpieces, and I could hear Isabella's voice clearly, even if she spoke in a whisper.

She adjusted her little black dress to ensure maximum impact. Her golden hair cascaded over a curve-hugging dress that screamed both danger and temptation. She showed more of those well-sculpted dancers' legs than was appropriate.

"Ready?" she asked, taking my arm.

"Let's do this," I replied, my pulse quickening.

As we stepped through the entrance of the auction warehouse, its nondescript exterior gave way to a realm that felt like another world. The dimly lit interior was charged with a palpable tension that mingled with an air of luxury. My eyes quickly adjusted to the low light, taking in the sight of heavy guards who stood like silent sentinels, their stern gazes sweeping over the crowd with an unspoken warning.

Around me, the warehouse buzzed with an uneasy energy. Wealthy men, their suits as sharp as their scrutinizing eyes, navigated through the crowd with a sense of entitlement that spoke of power and danger. Women of stunning beauty moved at their sides with a grace that seemed almost rehearsed, their laughter echoing softly in the vast space.

In the shadowy corners, figures engaged in hushed, urgent conversations. The subtle tilt of their heads, the discreet exchange of glances – these were the signs of the underworld, a silent language of the unspoken and the dangerous.

The air was a heady mix of expensive cologne and the warehouse's inherent mustiness, creating an alluring and foreboding atmosphere. I could sense the undercurrents of the room, the unspoken transactions, the veiled threats. This was a place where power was the currency and every word and gesture was part of a larger game. I knew I had to tread carefully, my senses alert to the hidden dangers that lurked beneath the surface.

"Remember," Isabella whispered, her breath warm against my ear, "we're here for Elena."

"Right," I agreed, trying to focus on the task at hand while resisting the urge to explore the tantalizing contours of her body. "Let's split up and see what we can learn."

I moved through the crowd, engaging in light conversation while keeping an eye out for any signs of Elena. The auction was set to begin soon, and I could feel the anticipation building like a slow burn, igniting my senses as I searched for our quarry.

"Have you found anything?" Isabella murmured into the tiny microphone hidden within her necklace. Her voice was like silk, smooth and seductive, threatening to unravel the tightly wound knot of self-control I clung to.

"Nothing yet," I replied, my eyes scanning the room as the auctioneer took his place behind the podium. "Stay sharp."

"Always," she purred, her tone suggesting she was enjoying this game of cat and mouse far more than I dared to admit.

I stood rigid, my senses heightened, as the auctioneer stepped forward, commanding the room's attention. His voice, authoritative and clear, cut through the murmurs and chatter, demanding silence. The crowd stilled, a mix of anticipation and greed hanging thick in the air. I glanced at Isabella beside me, her expression a mask of controlled disgust.

The auction was unlike any I had seen before – exclusive, illicit, and deeply unsettling. Opulent chandeliers cast a soft glow over the room, illuminating faces that held no hint of conscience. I could feel the weight of wealth and power in the air, a tangible force that seemed to suffocate all sense of morality.

The auctioneer's voice boomed again, announcing the first item. My stomach churned as a young girl, no more than eighteen, was led onto the stage by a hulking henchman. She was from Belarus, the auctioneer proclaimed, his tone dehumanizing as he described her like one would an object of art. Clad in nothing but lingerie and heels, she looked terrified, her vulnerability stark against the backdrop of the leering crowd.

"Blonde hair, blue eyes, a true beauty," the auctioneer continued, appraising her features and traits as if she were a prized mare. I felt a surge of anger, tinged with a helplessness that was unfamiliar to me.

Isabella leaned in, her voice low. "This is sickening, Luigi. How can they just...?"

"I know," I murmured back, my eyes not leaving the stage. "But we have to stay focused. We're here for Elena."

The girl on the stage was trembling now, her eyes downcast. The auctioneer rambled on about her youth and her innocence as if these were merely attributes to raise her price.

Bids started to fly from the room's shadowy corners, each one a stark reminder of the depravity that surrounded us. I clenched my fists, the urge to intervene, to put an end to this grotesque display, growing stronger by the second.

Isabella's hand found mine, her grip tight. "Luigi, we can't blow our cover. Not yet."

She was right. As much as every fiber of my being screamed to act, our mission was to find Elena. Any rash move now could jeopardize everything.

"We wait," I agreed, though the words tasted like

bile in my mouth. "But once we find Elena, we bring this whole operation down."

The girl was led off the stage, her fate sealed by the highest bidder – nine thousand Euros. A chill ran down my spine as I thought of Elena, wondering if she, too, had faced such a terrifying ordeal.

The auction continued, each "item" presented evoking the same mix of anger and despair in me. I watched every nerve on edge, waiting for any sign of Elena. This was a world I thought I understood, a world of shadows and crime, but what I saw that night was a darkness beyond anything I had encountered. It was a darkness that ate away at the soul, leaving nothing but a void where humanity should have been.

Isabella and I exchanged a look, a silent pact forming between us. We would find Elena, and we would end this nightmare. No matter what it took.

"I'll make my way toward the stage," I said. "Why don't you look around."

Isabella squeezed my hand in a silent confirmation.

The auctioneer's voice, a practiced purr, slithered through the opulent air. I caught sight of a familiar face at the bar. My pulse quickened like a staccato drumbeat, pounding in my ears as his black eyes locked onto mine with a predatory intensity.

"Isabella," I murmured into the hidden microphone, "we've got company."

"Where?" she asked, her voice a tempting caress that coiled around my resolve like a velvet noose.

"By the bar," I replied tersely, struggling to maintain my composure amid the mounting threat. "It's the brute that knocked me out cold yesterday." The Rimini henchman was unmistakable, a brutish silhouette born of shadows and malice.

"Understood," she whispered, sultry determination lacing her words as we both continued our ruse.

I sauntered over to the bar, feigning disinterest in the henchman while ordering a gin with a twist of lime. As the bartender slid the cool glass across the polished counter, I felt the weight of the henchman's stare against my back like a brand.

"Nice night for an auction, isn't it?" I asked the barman, my voice casual but laden with unspoken meaning.

The man grunted noncommittally, replacing the gin bottle with its green and gray label.

"Do you usually work at these events?" I continued.

"None of your business," he growled, releasing my gaze with a dismissive flick as his eyes darted along the bar, searching for other customers.

"Fair enough," I shrugged, taking another sip of gin. "Just thought I'd be friendly."

"Friendliness will get you killed in this line of work," he sneered, moving over to an elderly man at the other end of the bar.

"Stay alert," I warned Isabella as I returned to our mission, scouring the crowd for any trace of Elena. "We're being watched."

"Understood," she whispered, her voice a smoky promise that sent shivers down my spine despite the danger closing in around us. Together, we navigated the treacherous waters of temptation and secrecy, determined to find Elena before it was too late.

"Lot number seventeen," the auctioneer droned, his voice a dispassionate monotone that belied the perverse nature of his wares. "A young woman from Eastern Europe, trained in the arts of dance and seduction."

"Could it be her?" Isabella murmured in my ear. I swallowed hard, my mouth suddenly dry as the desert sands of Egypt.

"Let's not jump to conclusions," I replied, my voice low and measured. "We need to be certain before we make our move."

"Agreed," she whispered.

A young woman was led onto the stage, a brunette with a haunted look in her eyes. She was dressed only in heels and fishnet stockings, her vulnerability stark and unsettling amidst the sea of lecherous gazes. The dim lighting cast shadows over her slender frame, lending her an ethereal, almost ghostly appearance.

"Five thousand!" someone yelled.

"Observe the fluidity of her movements, the allure in her gaze," the auctioneer continued, his voice taking on a hypnotic rhythm. "A beauty trained in the art of dance, her every motion is poetry, her every look a siren's call."

The crowd murmured in approval, eyes fixed on the young woman as she tried to maintain a semblance of dignity under their scrutiny. The auctioneer, a master of his macabre craft, detailed her talents and allure, reducing her to an object of desire, a mere product to be consumed.

"Six thousand!" was heard from somewhere behind me.

I felt a pang of disgust and pity. This wasn't just an auction; it was a blatant display of human depravity. The young woman's presence on the stage was a stark reminder of the sinister world we had infiltrated – a world where human lives were traded like commodities and souls were auctioned to the highest bidder.

"Seven thousand," a new bidder called out, his voice slithering through the room like a serpent seeking its prey. I clenched my jaw, rage boiling beneath the surface as I gripped the edge of the table, knuckles turning white.

"Eight," another voice chimed in, raising the stakes even higher. I could see Isabella staring at the stage, her body coiled and ready to strike at a moment's notice.

"Ten thousand euros!" a voice boomed, cutting through the din like a knife through silk. The room fell silent, all eyes turning toward the bidder as though drawn by some magnetic force. My pulse quickened, a bead of sweat trickling down the back of my neck as I realized the implications of what was happening.

"Isabella," I murmured urgently into the hidden microphone, "it is time."

"Then let's make our move before it's too late," she urged her gaze momentarily locking into mine, the heat of her eyes searing into my very soul.

*

"Eleven thousand!" I yelled at the top of my lungs, drawing all attention to me.

At the very same time, a high, shrill scream was heard from the other side of the room as Isabella initiated her part.

"Get your hands off me!" she screamed with ferocious intensity, her voice laced with fury and indignation. She pointed accusingly at a man standing uncomfortably close to her. "This pervert just groped me!" she yelled, her face contorted with anger and violation.

The accused man, caught in the sudden spotlight of accusation, stammered a denial, his face turning a shade of guilty crimson. The crowd erupted into an uproar, the air instantly charged with anger and suspicion. Isabella's outburst had struck a nerve, turning the attention of the room onto the accused man as whispers and shocked expressions rippled through the gathered crowd.

In the midst of the turmoil, I found our chance. The focus of the room was now entirely on Isabella and her alleged assaulter, creating the perfect diversion.

With the crowd's attention diverted, I slipped out two small metal containers from my pocket. I pulled the pins and rolled them towards the sides of the room. The grenades burst into flames, and instantly, thick smoke billowed out, engulfing the room in a dense, impenetrable fog.

Panic ensued. Shouts and screams melded with the sound of scrambling feet. The cacophony of confusion drowned out the auctioneer's voice. I could barely make out figures through the smoke, shadows moving frantically in the haze.

I pushed my way through the disoriented crowd,

my eyes stinging and my heart pounding in my chest. Reaching the stage, I saw Elena, her eyes wide with fear. Grabbing her arm, I pulled her down, guiding her through the smoke-filled room.

"We have to move. Now!" I shouted over the noise, my voice barely audible. "I am a friend!"

We stumbled through the chaos, the outline of the exit barely visible. Bursting out into the cool night air, we ran towards the borrowed Lamborghini, its sleek form a beacon in the madness. I handed Elena my jacket as she wore nothing but the stockings and ushered her into the passenger seat. I slammed the door shut before jumping into the driver's seat.

As I revved the engine, the sound cut through the night like a promise of escape. We sped away, leaving the commotion of the auction and its dark dealings behind us, but men hurried out the warehouse door, aiming for motorcycles and vehicles. At that moment, every second felt like a small victory over the shadows we had left behind.

The night air was electric as I gunned the Lamborghini down the streets of Rimini, the engines roaring a fierce cry in the quiet. Beside me, Elena, half-naked and shivering, clutched the seat, her eyes wide with terror. The rearview mirror showed two motorcycles and a Jeep in hot pursuit, their headlights slicing through the darkness like predatory eyes.

"Hold on!" I yelled over the Lambo's growl. I swerved onto a narrower street, tires screeching against the cobblestone. The motorcycles were relentless, keeping pace, their riders masked and ominous. The Jeep lumbered behind, a hulking menace in the night.

Shots rang out, the sound shattering the air. Bullets whizzed past, one striking the Lamborghini's rear. I felt a jolt of adrenaline, my grip tightening on the wheel. Another turn, a narrow miss with a streetlight. I could almost feel the bikers' breath on our necks.

Elena was screaming now, a sound lost in the chaos. I glanced at her, her face a portrait of fear and determination.

"I won't let them get us," I promised, more to myself than to her.

The streets of Rimini became a blur, each turn a calculated risk. I darted down alleys across junctions, the Lamborghini responding like a living thing under my hands. The bikers were skilled, their movements synchronized, but I had one advantage – I knew these streets like the back of my hand.

A plan formed in my mind. I headed towards the outskirts, where the roads were less predictable and more dangerous. The bikers followed – their engines a relentless drone. The Jeep struggled to keep up, its bulk less suited to the tight turns and sudden drops.

Then, a chance – a narrow alley, barely visible. I took it, the Lamborghini's sides scraping against the walls. The first biker attempted to follow but misjudged the turn, crashing into the wall with a sickening crunch. The second hesitated, then accelerated, determined not to lose us.

The alley opened onto a wider road, and the path was clear for a moment. Then, out of nowhere, a truck turned onto the road, its driver unaware of the drama unfolding. The second biker swerved, narrowly avoiding a collision but losing control. His bike skidded, throwing him onto the road.

The Jeep was still behind us, but its presence was less menacing now, more desperate. I pushed the Lamborghini harder, feeling every horsepower straining beneath the hood.

Then, salvation – the sound of sirens, blue and red lights flashing in the distance. The police. The Jeep slowed, then turned, disappearing into the night.

I didn't stop until the lights of San Marino rose before us, a beacon of safety. I drove through the quiet streets, each turn taking us further from the nightmare we'd just escaped.

As I pulled up outside my place, the engine ticking as it cooled, Elena finally spoke, her voice a whisper. "Is it over?"

I looked at her, at the bruises forming, the terror still lingering in her eyes. "For now," I said, my voice steady. "For now, it's over."

But I knew the danger was far from over, and I could not shake the feeling that our enemies were still lurking in the darkness, waiting for the perfect moment to strike. We may have evaded them for now, but the game was only just beginning. And in the end, only one side would emerge victorious.

6

The Lamborghini roared to a halt outside Caterina's apartment building, a quaint structure nestled in the heart of the city. I felt the tension melt from my shoulders as I surveyed the familiar surroundings. This was a sanctuary, a place where we could catch our breath and buy some time.

"Come on," I said to Elena, guiding her through the dimly lit entrance. Our footsteps echoed along the narrow corridor, each step bringing us closer to safety.

We reached Caterina's door, and I knocked gently, hoping she wouldn't mind the unexpected intrusion. When the door swung open, my heart skipped a beat. She welcomed us warmly into her home, her dark eyes filled with concern for our well-being.

"Luigi, my dear. You look like you've seen better days. Come in, come in."

Caterina's apartment was a haven amidst the chaos that swirled around us. The ambiance was a blend of contemporary charm and warm hospitality. Soft, ambient lighting accentuated the open, airy space, where a grand piano stood as a centerpiece, its sleek silhouette a testament to her refined taste. The walls, minimalist yet inviting, were adorned with an array of photographs capturing Caterina's travels and treasured moments, each frame a window into her world.

The decor was light and homely, with subtle touches of elegance evident in the carefully chosen furnishings.

Instead of antique trinkets, the shelves and surfaces were adorned with a few select pieces of modern art and decorative items, each reflecting Caterina's flair for contemporary style.

The rich aroma of ragù filled the air, but I was certain it wasn't Caterina who had prepared it. Signora Ricci, a neighbor known for her culinary skills, often sent up dishes to Caterina, ensuring that her kitchen was always infused with the scents of traditional Italian cooking. This evening was no exception, and the fragrance of the hearty sauce stirred a hunger in me, reminding me of the comforts of home and the simple pleasures of a well-cooked meal.

"Please, make yourselves comfortable," Caterina said, gesturing toward the plush sofa that dominated her cozy living room. Its cushions called out to me, offering solace from the relentless events that had led us here.

Elena hesitated, clearly feeling out of place in this foreign environment. I placed a reassuring hand on her shoulder, urging her to take a seat. As we settled into the comforting embrace of the sofa, I caught a glimpse of the colorful tapestry that hung above the fireplace. It depicted San Marino's storied history, a testament to the resilience and strength of its people.

"Thank you for letting us in," I said quietly, my gratitude genuine. "We needed a safe place to stay, at least for tonight."

"Of course, Luigi," Caterina replied, her voice soft and soothing. "You're always welcome here. And your friend... Elena, is it? She's welcome, too."

I glanced over at Elena, who was studying the room with wide, curious eyes. The warmth of Caterina's home seemed to have worked its magic on her as well; the nervous tension had faded from her shoulders, replaced by a cautious sense of ease.

"Stay as long as you need," Caterina continued, her words breathing life into the flickering embers of hope within me. "We'll figure this out together."

In this sanctuary, surrounded by the echoes of a thousand stories and the promise of safety, we would find a way to confront the darkness that pursued us and emerge stronger for it.

"Come with me, Elena," Caterina beckoned as she led the young woman down a narrow hallway adorned with exquisite artwork. "I have some clothes you can borrow."

"Thank you, Caterina," Elena replied, her voice barely audible in our hushed atmosphere.

I watched them disappear, and my thoughts wandered to the sensual curve of Elena's hips, the delicate arch of her back. I shook my head, reining in my desires, and reminded myself of the danger we were facing.

When they returned, Elena was transformed. She was draped in a simple black dress that clung to her like a second skin, subtly highlighting her fit dancer's physique. The fabric seemed to move with her, each step a testament to her physical strength and grace. At that moment, I couldn't help but notice the stark contrast between her and Caterina. While Caterina carried the elegance that comes with experience and age, Elena's form exuded a different kind of allure – one born of youth and vitality. Her green eyes sparkled a vibrant mix of gratitude and lingering unease, reminding me of the relentless passage of time and its subtle transformations.

"Much better," Caterina said, appraising Elena with a smile. "Now, let's sit and talk."

"Indeed," I agreed, gesturing for them to join me at the small table nestled in the corner of the living room. The soft glow of the candles flickering against the walls seemed to heighten the intimacy of the moment, their shadows playing out an ancient dance of seduction and secrecy.

"Listen carefully, Elena," I began, my voice steady and serious. "We are not out of danger yet. There are people who would do anything to find you, and they won't hesitate to hurt those who stand in their way."

Her eyes widened, fear threading its way through her gaze. "But why? I don't understand."

"Neither do I," I admitted, running a hand through my hair. "But we must remain cautious, vigilant. Trust no one, and keep our whereabouts a secret."

"Can we trust Caterina?" Elena asked, glancing over at the older woman.

"Si, Elena," I replied. "Caterina is one of the few people I trust with my life."

"Very well." She took a deep breath, her chest swelling beneath the fabric of the dress. "What now?"

"First, we rest," I said, my voice low and reassuring. "Tomorrow, I'll devise a plan to keep you safe and uncover the truth behind all of this."

As I spoke those words, a spark of determination ignited in her eyes just as the candlelight continued to cast its seductive glow upon the room. It was at that moment that I realized just how much of a challenge it would be to resist temptation's call while still protecting Elena from the darkness that threatened to consume us both.

*

The following morning, I left Elena in Caterina's care and stepped out into the crisp San Marino air. The scent of fresh espresso wafted from a nearby café, mingling with the faint aroma of dew-kissed cobblestones. It was a fleeting moment of tranquility before the storm that awaited me.

I pulled my phone from my pocket and dialed Mr. Popescu's number. As it rang, I couldn't help but imagine the relief that would flood his voice when he heard the news.

"Signor Ferro?" His voice trembled on the other end, an anxious question hanging in the air.

"Mr. Popescu," I replied with a reassuring tone. "Your daughter is safe."

"God bless you, Signor Ferro," he breathed, audibly choking back tears. "I owe you everything."

"Your gratitude is enough," I said, my heart swelling with pride at my small victory. "But we are not done yet. I will bring her to you once we've ensured her safety."

"Thank you," he whispered, the raw emotion in

his voice a testament to the bond between father and daughter.

With that, I ended the call and made my way to my office. As I turned the corner, my Vespa came into view, gleaming in the sunlight like a beacon of hope amidst the uncertainty. But as I approached my office door, I found it ajar.

My heart raced as I pushed it open, revealing a scene of devastation. The room was ransacked – papers strewn across the floor, drawers upended, and files scattered like leaves in a tempest. The violation bore down on me like the weight of the world, crushing my spirit with each step I took through the wreckage.

They had been here, searching for something – or someone. Every aspect of my life was picked apart, leaving me exposed and vulnerable. I felt as if a thousand eyes bore into my soul, scrutinizing my every move.

Anger surged through me like a torrent, fueling my desire for justice and retribution. It was not only my life that had been invaded but the lives of Mr. Popescu and his daughter. Their safety depended on my ability to decipher the intentions of those who sought their harm.

I spent hours sifting through the debris, searching for any clue that might lead me to the perpetrators. But even amidst the chaos, one thing became clear: whatever they were after, they hadn't found it.

Then, a realization hit me over the head like a sledgehammer. They were not after something. They were after me and my address.

With haste, I ran over to my apartment, just a few

streets down. I stopped short in front of the door. It was just as open as I had found the office door. I drew my gun and carefully kicked the door open, pointing the gun at whatever I may find.

"Merda," I muttered under my breath, finding my home in the same state as the office. My living room, once an organized oasis amidst the tumultuous storm of the city, now resembled a battlefield strewn with casualties – torn papers, shattered glass, and overturned trinkets.

My eyes caught a glimpse of something clearly placed on the table. It was a note hastily scrawled in an unfamiliar hand. "We have Isabella," it read. "You'll never see her again."

My heart thudded against my ribcage, adrenaline coursing through my veins. The stakes were higher than I'd anticipated; not only did I need to get Elena to safety, but now Isabella's life was hanging in the balance as well.

"Isabella… Dio mio," I whispered, anger morphing into steely determination. As I clutched the note tightly in my fist, memories of past cases flickered through my mind like scenes from an old black-and-white film. I remembered the faces of those I'd saved and the ones I'd lost, the weight of their lives forever etched into my soul.

I thought of the men who had visited the auction yesterday, the depths of human depravity, and the unbreakable spirit of those who refuse to be broken.

I felt the familiar fire of conviction ignite within me as I recalled the countless times I'd stared danger in the face and emerged victorious. I had faced demons in both man and beast and whatever twisted soul was responsible for this carnage would be no different.

I had to get organized, and the first priority was Elena. I returned to Caterina's.

The afternoon sun cast a warm glow over San Marino. I had arranged for Elena to meet her father in a small park nestled beneath the ancient city walls. The air was thick with the scent of blooming jasmine, and the gentle hum of evening prayers from a nearby church mingled with the laughter of children playing.

"Are you ready?" I asked Elena as she stood beside me, her eyes flitting nervously around the park. She looked like a beautiful bird caught in a storm, desperate for shelter.

"Si, Luigi," she whispered. "I just... I never thought I would see him again."

"You will be safe now, Elena," I reassured her. "Your father would go to the ends of the earth to make sure you were safe."

As if on cue, Mr. Popescu appeared at the edge of the park, his eyes scanning the area with a frantic urgency. The moment they landed on his daughter, his entire being seemed to light up from within. He rushed towards her, arms outstretched, and Elena ran to meet him, tears streaming down her face.

"Elena!" Mr. Popescu cried, his voice cracking with emotion as he enfolded his daughter in a fierce embrace. For a moment, the chaos and danger that surrounded us evaporated, replaced by the simple joy of a father and daughter reunited.

"Thank you, Luigi," Elena choked out between sobs. "I owe you everything."

"Your safety is all the thanks I need," I replied softly, watching the loving tableau unfold before me. Yet behind my words, a gnawing dread tugged at my insides, reminding me that our mission was far from over.

"Signor Ferro," Mr. Popescu said, extending a calloused hand to grasp mine. "Words cannot express my gratitude. You are a true hero." He pressed the thick envelope with his life savings to my chest.

"We are not out of the woods yet," I said, my jaw tightening. "We still have work to do."

"Of course," Mr. Popescu nodded, his eyes clouded with concern. He turned to Elena, his voice gentle but firm. "I will take you somewhere safe now, darling."

"Good luck finding her, Luigi," Elena implored, her green eyes shining with determination. I could see the fear in her gaze, but beneath it lay a fierce courage that burned like a flame.

"I will find her," I told her, and as I watched Mr. Popescu lead his daughter away from the park, I felt the weight of that vow settle on my shoulders like a mantle. The shadows of night began to lengthen, whispering of secrets yet to be discovered and battles yet to be fought. As I turned to face the darkness, I knew I would not rest until Isabella was safely in my arms again.

As Mr. Popescu and Elena disappeared from sight, I felt a storm brewing in my mind. I needed a plan—a risky one that would outsmart these traffickers who had dared to cross me and threaten the lives of innocent people.

"Think, Ferro," I muttered to myself. "You've been in tighter spots before."

My mind wandered back to past cases, each a labyrinthine puzzle that tested the limits of my cunning and resourcefulness. But this time, the stakes were higher, the danger more personal. Isabella's life hung in the balance, and I knew that I couldn't afford any mistakes.

I began to formulate a plan, drawing upon years of experience in navigating the treacherous underbelly of this world. It was risky, but I couldn't shake the feeling that fortune favored the bold.

First, I paid a visit to an old friend—a former informant with connections to the criminal underworld. He owed me a favor, and tonight, I intended to collect. His small apartment reeked of desperation and cheap cologne, a testament to the life he'd chosen. I laid out my plan with the precision of a master chess player, expertly concealing my true intentions beneath a veneer of nonchalance.

"Are you sure about this, Luigi?" he asked nervously, his eyes darting around the room as if seeking an escape.

"Absolutely," I replied, my voice cold and steady. "And remember, this stays between us."

He nodded, sweat beading on his brow.

"Buona fortuna," he whispered, handing me a small package wrapped in brown paper. I took it without a word and left him to his sordid existence, a pawn in my grand game.

I spent the remainder of the night gathering tools and information, my senses heightened by the allure of danger and the tantalizing prospect of vengeance. I knew that I was walking a tightrope between life and death, each step taking me closer to the edge. But there was no turning back now—not with Isabella's fate hanging in the balance.

As dawn broke over the Adriatic sea, I found myself heading for a grand villa in Rimini. The Vespa purred beneath me, a loyal steed carrying its rider toward destiny or destruction. My thoughts danced between the two, a tango of anticipation and dread.

The engine's purr died down as I beheld the shadowy structure, its unassuming facade concealing the darkness within. This was the place where innocence was stolen, where souls were devoured by the ravenous maw of greed.

"Time to face the devil," I whispered, my breath condensing in the cold air.

My fingers tightened around the package I had acquired earlier, its contents vital to my plan.

As I approached the imposing building, the door opened, revealing a statuesque woman in a blood-red dress. Her eyes, as black as the abyss, studied me with predatory hunger, her lips curling into a sinister smile.

"Signor Ferro," she purred, her voice dripping with the venom of temptation. "We've been expecting you."

The air around me crackled with danger, an electrifying tension that threatened to shatter the fragile balance between life and death. My every instinct screamed at me to turn back, but my heart thundered on, fueled by my determination to save Isabella...and perhaps myself.

"Your invitation must have been lost in the mail," I retorted, my tone icy and unwavering.

"Come in," she beckoned, her voice sultry and smooth as silk. "Let's see what you're made of."

The door closed behind me.

7

The woman led me through the villa's opulent hallways, each adorned with frescoes that whispered of a time gone by. She moved with the grace of a panther, predatory and alluring. It was hard not to admire her beauty, but I reminded myself she was part of the very underworld I sought to dismantle.

Her heels clicked against the marble floor, echoing in the vast spaces like a metronome set to the rhythm of my racing heart. I couldn't help but notice how her dress clung to every curve like honey dripping down a spoon.

Inside, the villa's opulence was undeniable, a testament to the power and wealth amassed by those who dwelt within its walls. Marble floors gleamed underfoot, and the walls were adorned with priceless works of art. I committed every detail to memory, taking careful note of each room's layout and the positions of those who lingered in the shadows.

"Quite the home you've got here," I remarked as we passed an intricate mosaic depicting the Roman conquests.

"Only the best for our... esteemed guests," she purred, her voice sultry and enticing. "We do enjoy providing a touch of luxury for those who appreciate it."

I could feel her eyes on me, probing, searching for any weakness she could exploit. But I was no stranger to this dance and wouldn't be drawn off course.

"Ah, the salon," she announced, gesturing toward a room filled with plush velvet sofas and gleaming mahogany tables. "This is where we entertain, where deals are made and alliances forged."

"An impressive stage indeed," I replied, feigning admiration.

"Ah," she replied, her eyes never leaving mine. "And are you easily seduced by beauty?"

"Only when it comes wrapped in a mystery," I confessed, feeling the pull of desire tugging at my resolve. She was a dangerous game, and I was perilously close to being caught in her web.

"Then you've come to the right place," she whispered, her lips curving into a predatory smile. "There's so much more to discover."

"Indeed," I murmured, my mind racing with the possibilities that lay before me. The woman was a riddle, and I intended to solve her, to unravel the secrets she held so closely to her chest.

As she turned away to point out another feature, I seized the moment. I slipped the parcel from my pocket – a sophisticated listening device and a 360 infrared camera. My fingers moved deftly, activating the devices and ensuring they were transmitting live audio and video to the police stationed outside. When I discussed this with Commissario Carlotto last night, he had been very specific about getting solid evidence against this elusive group of individuals.

With a final glance around, I placed the parcel on a table at the center of the room, its innocuous appearance belying the power it held.

"Something wrong, Signor Ferro?" she asked, an edge of suspicion creeping into her voice.

"Nothing at all," I replied, fixing a smile on my lips. "I'm simply… admiring your taste in decor."

"Is that all?" Her gaze lingered on the parcel, but her expression remained unreadable.

"Indeed," I said, forcing a laugh. "I have an eye for beauty in all its forms."

"Then you must be enjoying this view," she retorted, with a wicked smile playing on her lips. The tension between us was almost palpable, like the charged air before a thunderstorm.

"Immensely," I replied, my voice steady and my eyes locked on hers. The game was far from over, and my resolve would not waver. For beneath the veneer of seduction and desire, a darker truth lay hidden – one that I was determined to unveil.

The scent of her perfume hung heavy in the air, a heady blend of jasmine and something darker, more primal. She leaned closer, her lush lips mere inches from my ear as she whispered, "And what do you think of our little operation here, Signor Ferro?"

"Quite atrocious," I replied, my voice measured and cool, though my heart raced beneath my tailored suit. "But you probably have another angle to the true nature of your business, don't you?"

"Curiosity killed the cat, they say." Her laughter tinkled like the delicate chime of glass, but there was a coldness to it that sent shivers down my spine.

"True, but some cats have nine lives," I quipped, a thinly veiled challenge dancing in my eyes. "Tell me, bella, what exactly is it that you're trafficking here? Surely not just luxury goods, art, and fine wines."

Her gaze hardened instantly, a subtle warning that I had crossed a line. "You ask a lot of questions, Signor Ferro."

I shrugged.

"Are you a collector?" she continued, pausing beside an antique cabinet filled with delicate porcelain figurines. Her long, slender fingers traced their intricate patterns, leaving a trail of shivers in their wake.

"Of sorts," I answered enigmatically, the corners of my mouth turning up in a wry grin. "I collect stories, unraveling the threads that bind us to our baser instincts."

"Stories," she repeated, her gaze never wavering from mine. "And what story do you hope to find here?"

"We'll see," I replied, feeling the thrill of the chase coursing through my veins. "But I'm certain it will be one worth telling."

The woman's gaze shifted as she fixed her eyes on me.

"Mr. Ferro, your little escapade with Elena has cost us greatly. She was our most prized asset," she hissed.

I squared my shoulders, meeting her icy gaze.

"Elena is not an asset. She's a person, and she's safe from you now. But we're not done here. Where's Isabella?"

Her lips curled into a sardonic smile. "Isabella? A mere pawn and now a liability, thanks to you. Her fate will compensate for our losses from Elena's absence."

Rage boiled within me, my hands balled into fists.

"You won't be selling anyone. Not Isabella, not anyone else. This ends here."

"Oh, Ferro," she sneered, "you seem to misunderstand your position here."

It was a stalemate, each word ratcheting the tension higher. I knew I had to act quickly. I faced the statuesque woman, her cold eyes trying to pierce my facade.

"You know," I began casually, a hint of nonchalance in my voice as I eyed a painting on the wall, "this piece reminds me of a masterwork of Caravaggio. Do you appreciate his work?" I asked my tone light but laced with a hidden urgency.

She raised an eyebrow, thrown off by the sudden shift in conversation. "Caravaggio? I prefer more… contemporary art. Why do we speak of paintings now, Mr. Ferro?" Her suspicion was evident, but she entertained my diversion.

"I've always found his use of chiaroscuro intriguing," I continued, my eyes briefly meeting hers before shifting back to the painting. "Particularly in his piece, 'Tempesta'," I added, emphasizing the last word. That was the secret signal for Carlotto to engage. I just hoped they had heard and seen everything that had happened over the last few minutes.

As soon as the word left my lips, the villa erupted into a cacophony of chaos. Doors were violently thrust open as Commissario Carlotto and his team stormed the grand hall, their shouts of authority cutting through the thick air.

The traffickers, momentarily stunned by the abrupt

intrusion, scrambled in a disorganized frenzy. Panic overtook the room as they desperately sought escape routes or grabbed weapons in a futile attempt to resist.

"Police! Don't move!" Carlotto bellowed, his team swiftly moving into position, weapons trained on the traffickers.

The statuesque woman, her composure shattered, looked at me with a mix of betrayal and realization. "You called the cops?" she spat, her voice venomous.

"As any concerned citizen," I replied coolly, stepping back as the police swarmed the room, efficiently apprehending the traffickers.

Carlotto made his way through the chaos towards us, his gaze fixed on the woman.

"We have been watching you for a long time. You're under arrest for human trafficking and other related charges," he declared, his voice unwavering.

As the woman was handcuffed, a sudden movement caught my eye. One of the traffickers had evaded the initial roundup and was now pointing a gun at Carlotto, his hand shaking.

Without a moment's hesitation, I lunged toward Carlotto, pushing him out of the line of fire just as the gun went off. The bullet whizzed past us, embedding itself in the lavish decor.

In an instant, Carlotto's team subdued the gunman, their trained efficiency evident in every move. Carlotto, recovering from the near miss, gave me a nod of gratitude.

"You have a knack for finding trouble, Ferro," he

said, a hint of a smile breaking through his usually stern demeanor.

"Seems to be my calling," I replied, watching as the police secured the room, but elsewhere the battle continued.

The villa, once a symbol of illicit luxury, had transformed into a battleground. The air was thick with tension, gunshots punctuating the chaos like a deadly rhythm. Amidst the uproar, my focus narrowed to a single objective: finding Isabella. My heart raced, adrenaline surging through my veins as I navigated the labyrinth of violence.

I ducked as a fist flew towards me, feeling the whoosh of air as it narrowly missed. My response was instinctive; a swift jab connected with my assailant's jaw, sending him staggering back. I pushed forward, my senses hyper-alert, every nerve attuned to the unfolding anarchy.

The room spun with a maelstrom of bodies – traffickers, their henchmen, and Carlotto's police force clashing in a fierce melee. I sidestepped a lunging attacker, grabbing his arm and twisting it behind his back, using his momentum to propel him into another adversary. They collapsed in a heap, momentarily clearing my path.

Through the chaos, I caught a glimpse of movement – a group of henchmen dragging a bound figure away from the fray. It was Isabella. Anguish and determination flooded me in equal measure. I surged towards them, my resolve steeling me against the pandemonium.

As I approached, one of the henchmen spotted me. He raised his gun, but I was quicker. I lunged, tackling him to the ground. The gun skittered across the marble floor. Blows were exchanged, the fight brutal and unrelenting. I could feel the impact of each hit, but I couldn't stop – not when Isabella's life hung in the balance.

I dispatched the first henchman with a well-placed punch and turned just in time to block a strike from the second. Our struggle was fierce; he was strong, but desperation lent me strength. I could hear Isabella's muffled cries, spurring me on.

A third henchman joined the fray, swinging a heavy lamp at me. I ducked, feeling the rush of air as the lamp smashed into the wall. Shards of glass flew, glinting like deadly rain in the villa's abundant light.

I kicked out, catching the third henchman in the stomach. He doubled over, gasping. The second henchman took advantage of my divided attention, landing a solid punch. Pain exploded in my jaw, but it only fueled my resolve.

I fought back with a barrage of punches, each one a promise of retribution for Isabella. Finally, the second henchman crumpled to the ground, unconscious.

Breathing heavily, I turned to the third henchman. He was trying to crawl away, but I grabbed him, hauling him to his feet. With a swift movement, I disarmed him, throwing him into the chaos of the ongoing battle.

"Isabella!" I called out, slicing through her bindings,

our eyes meeting in a silent exchange of trust and unspoken words.

"Luigi!" Her voice was filled with relief and pain. I wrapped my arm around her, guiding her through the pandemonium and back towards the entrance.

"We need to get out of here," I said, my voice barely audible over the din.

Together, we navigated through the chaos, dodging combatants and debris. Each step was a fight for survival, the villa a maze of danger and desperation.

As we neared the entrance, a sudden explosion rocked the villa. A flash of fire blinded us even in broad daylight, and for a moment, everything seemed to pause. The shockwave hit us, knocking us off our feet. I shielded Isabella with my body as debris rained down.

The world was a blur of smoke and screams. I rose unsteadily, pulling Isabella up with me.

"Follow me," I urged her, my heart pounding in time with our rapid footsteps.

"Luigi," she gasped, her voice strained as we raced through the dimly lit kitchen, dodging overturned pots and pans. "There are more girls in here..."

"We'll get them later," I reassured her, my determination unwavering as we reached the side door, the faint scent of rosemary wafting through the air.

"Stop!" a voice boomed behind us, and we froze; our escape momentarily halted. Turning, I found myself staring down the barrel of a gun held by a man whose eyes burned with hatred.

"Drop your weapons," he snarled, and reluctantly,

we complied, our hands raised in surrender. But I knew this was far from over.

"Hey, pal," I began, my tone deceptively calm as I weighed our options. "We both know how this ends."

"Your death?" he spat, his finger tightening on the trigger.

"No," I countered, my voice sharpening like a stiletto. "Your downfall."

"Enough talk!" he growled, but before he could react, I lunged forward, wrenching the gun from his grasp and sending him sprawling to the floor.

"Run!" I shouted at Isabella, my heart hammering in my chest as we stumbled towards the exit, each step a triumph over the horrors we'd left behind.

Outside, the Rimini sunshine was a stark contrast to the inferno we'd escaped. Sirens wailed in the distance, the flashing lights of police cars painting the facade in shades of blue and red.

We had made it out. We were alive. But as we stood there, catching our breaths, the gravity of what had transpired hit us. The villa, now a smoldering ruin, was a testament to the night's harrowing ordeal.

"Luigi," Isabella panted, her eyes wide with fear and exhilaration. "We did it, but what of the others?"

At that moment, amidst the chaos and the relief, I knew that this was more than just a mission accomplished. It was a testament to the resilience of the human spirit and the relentless pursuit of justice.

Carlotto approached his expression a mix of relief and resolve.

"We've got them, Ferro. It's over."

I nodded, my gaze on Isabella, who leaned against me, her breaths ragged but safe in my arms. Once a bastion of illicit terror, the villa was now a scene of triumph and justice.

The morning had been a tempest of suspense and action, but as the dust settled, I knew we had struck a blow against the darkness. We had saved Isabella and dismantled a ring of horror. As we stood amidst the aftermath, the weight of our actions and their far-reaching consequences settled upon us, a reminder of the cost and the necessity of our fight.

We sat down on a low garden wall. Medics were looking over Isabella and attended to a cut on my right cheek.

"Luigi," Isabella whispered, her dark eyes shimmering with unshed tears. "Look."

My gaze followed hers to where a young woman, her cheeks streaked with dirt and tears, clung to her mother like a lifeline, their cries forming a symphony of sorrow and solace. "Grazie," the woman sobbed over and over again, her grip tightening around her daughter's slender frame.

"Ragazza mia," her mother cooed, tenderly kissing her hair. "I found you."

"Now I see why you do this," Isabella murmured, leaning into my side. I felt the warmth of her body against mine, the subtle curve of her hips beneath the thin fabric of her dress, and my heart thudded with an intensity that belied the calm of our surroundings.

"I know," I said quietly, my fingertips tracing the

delicate line of her jaw. "But it's easy to forget this when we're in the midst of the fight."

"I'll never forget it," she promised, her voice thick with emotion.

A shiver ran down my spine as her breath ghosted over my skin, the scent of her perfume mingling with the faint aroma of gunpowder and sweat that still clung to us both. The world seemed to narrow down to just the two of us, our bodies tethered together by desire, temptation, and the knowledge of what we had achieved.

"I'm grateful for this win," I admitted, my voice a low rumble.

"And it's only the beginning," Isabella said, her eyes shining with determination.

Around us, families continued to reunite, their voices weaving together in a tapestry of hope and healing that seemed to shimmer in the air like the fading light. And as we stood there, our bodies pressed close, I knew that we had done more than just dismantle the trafficking ring; we had exposed the dark underbelly of our city's secrets, bringing them into the harsh light of day where they could no longer fester and thrive.

"It's time," I told her, my hand reaching for hers. "It's time to go home."

"Si," she agreed, her fingers slipping between mine as we stepped away from the villa, the weight of our victory settling around us like a cloak of shadows and starlight.

We arrived at my Vespa, its classic lines gleaming beneath the golden glow of the summer sun. As I helped Isabella onto the seat, I glanced back at the scene unfolding behind us. Police officers led the apprehended traffickers to their vehicles while other officers continued to escort the rescued victims out of the building. The sight of those reunions brought a warmth to my chest that even the finest gin with a twist of lime couldn't replicate.

The door to my office clicked shut, leaving me in the embrace of shadows and silence. I sank into my chair, the leather cool against my skin, embracing the solitude that enveloped me like a shroud. The room around me smelled of old paper and polished wood, a testament to the years spent within these walls.

I took a slow sip of my gin, the bite of the alcohol stinging my lips, the twist of lime cutting through the haze of thoughts that swirled around my mind. The events of the recent case played out before me like a movie on an endless loop; justice had been served, but at what cost? A profound mix of satisfaction and sorrow washed over me as I considered the dark facets of humanity I had encountered.

"Perché?" I whispered to the empty room, my voice barely audible. Why did they have to suffer? Images of all the victims that had been before this haunted me, their eyes filled with pain, pleading for salvation. The stark reality of human trafficking weighed heavily on my conscience, like a millstone around my neck.

The smooth surface of the tumbler cradled in my hand reflected my troubled gaze, a mirror to the world-weary soul hidden behind my sharp dresser exterior. I ran a hand through my dark hair, feeling the prickling stubble of my three-millimeter beard. This was who I was, Luigi Ferro, private detective of San Marino—a man caught between darkness and light, forever chasing shadows in search of truth.

"Diavolo!" I slammed my fist down on the desk, startling myself with the sudden explosion of emotion. The Vespa keychain that dangled from my keys shook violently, a symbol of the freedom I sought but could not find. My heart raced, a frenzy of conflicting emotions surging through my veins.

"Easy," I muttered to myself, trying to regain control. But the storm inside me refused to be tamed, an unyielding tempest of anger, guilt, and despair. The faces of those I had saved—Elena, Isabella, and countless others—flitted through my mind, each a testament to the difference I had made in their lives, yet each one also reminded of the darkness that still lurked in the shadows.

"It's not all up to me," I whispered, my voice choked with emotion. I couldn't do it all alone. But who could share this burden with me? Caterina, my on-again-off-again girlfriend, was a pillar of support, but there were times when even her warm embrace could not shield me from the harsh realities of this world.

The sun dipped below the horizon, casting my office into deeper shadow. In the fading light, I found a moment of clarity amidst the chaos within. My gaze fixated on the raindrops cascading down the windowpane, each one resembling the tears I wished to shed for the victims of this cruel world.

"Justice," I whispered into the void, feeling both satisfaction and sorrow at the thought. The recent case had been harrowing, its dark facets revealing humanity's ugliest side. Human trafficking – a blight on society that I had confronted head-on. It was a victory but a bitter one, leaving an aftertaste that lingered heavily within me.

I muttered, letting out a sigh as I swirled the ice cubes in my glass. I took a slow sip of the cold, sharp liquid, savoring the tangy lime against my tongue. For a fleeting moment, the bitterness of the gin mirrored the turmoil brewing inside me.

The faces of the victims haunted my thoughts, their eyes pleading for salvation from the depths of hell they'd found themselves in. The pain in my heart only grew stronger, as if someone were gripping it tightly, refusing to let go. A part of me longed for Caterina, her soft touch and soothing voice that had always managed to calm the storm within me. But not tonight – tonight, I would have to face the tempest alone.

"Focus, Ferro," I hissed into the emptiness, forcing my thoughts back to the task at hand. The storm outside mirrored the one inside me, but I knew that giving in to it would only mean losing myself completely.

I took another sip of my gin, allowing it to soothe my frayed nerves. My reflection in the rain-streaked window gazed back at me, the dark circles under my eyes a testament to the battles fought and won.

"Never forget why you do this, Luigi," I whispered into the emptiness, taking a deep breath and slowly exhaling as the room seemed to grow quieter, the shadows on the wall no longer menacing but familiar, like old friends.

"Never forget."

The moment I stepped into Caterina's apartment, the chaos of the outside world seemed to fade. Her sanctuary was a balm for my soul, a warm embrace that enveloped me in its gentle arms. The scent of her perfume lingered in the air like a whispered promise, and I felt my shoulders relax as I let the door click shut behind me.

"Luigi," she murmured, stepping out from the shadows, her dark hair cascading over one shoulder, her eyes soft with concern. "I've been so worried about you."

"Hey, bella," I replied, my voice hoarse with fatigue. I hesitated, unsure whether to approach or retreat, but her silence spoke volumes.

"Come here," she said quietly, opening her arms to me. I melted into her embrace, feeling the weight of the world lift off my shoulders. In her arms, I could forget the darkness I'd seen, if only for a little while.

"Tell me everything," she urged her voice a soothing balm to my frayed nerves. We sat on the couch, our bodies pressed close together, seeking solace and warmth from each other.

"Another case closed," I began, my voice barely above a whisper. "Justice served and lives saved..." I looked down at my hands, the fingers stained with the memories of the blood and dirt I had touched, and shuddered.

"Luigi, look at me," Caterina implored, lifting my chin to meet her gaze. "You're doing important work, even if it means facing the darkest parts of humanity. You're making a difference."

"Am I really, though?" I muttered, the doubt gnawing at me like a hungry beast. "What if it's never enough?"

"Then you keep fighting," she insisted, her voice unwavering. "You fight for those who can't, and you give them hope."

"Hope," I echoed, the word tasting foreign on my tongue. A glimmer of it ignited within me, fueled by Caterina's unwavering faith in me.

"Let me take care of you tonight," she whispered, her breath warm against my ear. "I know what you need." As she spoke, her fingers danced across my chest, unbuttoning my shirt with a practiced ease. The touch sent shivers down my spine, awakening a longing that had been buried beneath the weight of the case.

"Take me away from this, bella," I murmured, surrendering to her touch. Her lips met mine in a tender kiss that promised solace and escape, if only for tonight.

"Ti amo, Luigi," she breathed against my skin, her words weaving their way into my heart like a secret spell. In her arms, I found the strength to face another day, buoyed by the knowledge that I was not alone in this fight.

Together, we would find a way to conquer the darkness.

I awoke the next morning, feeling the weight of Caterina's arm draped across my chest and her warm breath against my neck. Her presence was a soothing balm to my weary soul, yet I knew that the comfort it provided was fleeting, like a candle flickering in the night. As I gently disentangled myself from her embrace, careful not to wake her, my thoughts returned to the case and its harrowing conclusion.

"Buongiorno, Luigi," she murmured, her voice thick with sleep as she stirred beside me.

"Buongiorno, bella," I replied softly, pressing a tender kiss on her forehead. "Rest now. I have matters to attend to."

"Important matters?" she asked, her eyes still closed as a small smile played on her lips.

"Indeed," I confirmed, sliding out of bed and pulling on my clothes, the fabric whispering secrets against my skin. "There is much work to be done."

"Very well," she sighed, rolling over and burying her face in the pillow as I left the room. The scent of espresso wafted through the apartment, calling my name like a siren's song, but I resisted its allure, knowing that I had more pressing concerns.

As I descended the stairs and stepped into the crisp morning air, a glimmer of sunlight caught my eye, reflecting off the polished chrome of my Vespa. It stood there, silent and unassuming, an emblem of the freedom and power I wielded as a private investigator. My mind swirled with memories of the risks I had faced and the lives I had touched; each thought melding together, forging a renewed sense of purpose within me.

"Signor Ferro!" called the postman, his voice cutting through my reverie as he approached. "I have something for you."

"Ah, grazie," I replied, taking the proffered envelope from his outstretched hand. My fingers traced the foreign stamps and postmarks, curiosity piquing as I recognized the sender's name: Elena Popescu.

Have a good day, Signor Ferro," the postman smiled, tipping his cap before continuing on his rounds.

"Likewise," I muttered absently, my attention now focused on the contents of the envelope. Slitting it open with my finger, I extracted a postcard that bore an image of Bucharest's historic architecture, the graceful curves and intricate detailing a testament to the city's rich cultural heritage.

I read Elena's words:

"Dear Signor Ferro, I have returned to Romania with my father, and we are both safe, thanks to you. Your courage and determination gave me a second chance at life, for which I will be eternally grateful. May you always find the strength to continue your noble work."

I smiled, folding the postcard and tucking it into my jacket pocket close to my heart. Each beat was a reminder of the power I possessed, the ability to change lives through my actions and choices. And as I straddled my Vespa and revved the engine, I knew that it was a power I would never relinquish, no matter the cost.

"Arrivederci, Caterina," I whispered, the wind carrying my words as I sped away, leaving behind the comfort of her embrace to face the challenges that lay ahead. For I was Luigi Ferro, private investigator, and my journey had to continue. For as long as there were those who needed my help, I would be there, a beacon in the shadows, a protector of the innocent, and a seeker of truth.

THE END

LUIGI FERRO
WILL RETURN

A Story from

Yesteryear's Stories Reflected Today
Yabot AB
www.yabot.se

9 789189 822450